New York Times bestselling author **Shirley Jump** didn't have the will-power to diet, nor the talent to master under-eye concealer, so she bowed out of a career in television and opted instead for a career where she could be paid to eat at her desk—writing. At first, seeking revenge on her children for their grocery store tantrums, she sold embarrassing essays about them to anthologies. However, it wasn't enough to feed her growing addiction to writing funny. So she turned to the world of romance novels, where messes are (usually) cleaned up before The End. In the worlds Shirley gets to create and control, the children listen to their parents, the husbands always remember holidays, and the housework is magically done by elves. Though she's thrilled to see her books in stores around the world, Shirley mostly writes because it gives her an excuse to avoid cleaning the toilets and helps feed her shoe habit. To learn more, visit her website at www.shirleyjump.com

Praise for Shirley Jump:

'BOARDROOM BRIDE AND GROOM is well plotted, and all of the characters are beautifully realised. While it's often humorous, keep some tissues handy too.'
—*Romantic Times BOOKreviews*

About SWEETHEART LOST AND FOUND
'This tale of rekindled love is right on target: a delightful start to this uplifting, marriage-orientated series [*The Wedding Planners*].'
—*Library Journal.com*

About *NYT* bestselling anthology
SUGAR AND SPICE
'Jump's office romance gives the collection a kick, with fiery writing.'
—*PublishersWeekly.com*

To my children. Every day with you is a precious gift, and I thank God for blessing me with two of the most wonderful children in the world.

CHAPTER ONE

HE CREPT silently into the bedroom, his footsteps muffled by the hearty drumbeat of a summer thunderstorm.

He raised the knife, pausing only long enough to delight in the quick flash of lightning that illuminated his victim's terrified face, before—

"Dalton, I need your help!"

Dalton Scott let out a curse. Then another one. His neighbor. Viola Winterberry, one of those people who needed favors like trick-or-treaters needed another chocolate bar, was somewhere downstairs.

Interrupting. Again.

"I'm working, Mrs. Winterberry. On the *book*," he called down.

"I know," she said, her voice rising in volume as she climbed the stairs toward his office, "but I have—"

"I'm on a deadline." He shouted the words, heavy on the hint-hint.

Actually, he was way past his deadline.

"But you have to—"

"And if I get disturbed, I lose my concentration." He'd told her that a hundred times, yet she still walked in uninvited. It was his own fault. He'd forgotten to lock the door after he retrieved the paper this morning.

He needed a guard dog. A big one.

Aw, hell. It wouldn't matter. His writing stunk, dog or not. Concentration or not. He'd already missed his deadline, ticked off his editor, nearly destroyed his career.

What else could go wrong?

"I have an *emergency*," Mrs. Winterberry said, poking her curly gray head into his office and into his line of vision. "I know you said not to bother you, but I'm desperate, Dalton. *Desperate*. You said anytime I needed a favor, you'd help me out."

She'd been desperate last week when she needed a cup of sugar from him so she could make her special raspberry cake. Desperate the week before when she needed him to come by immediately to change a lightbulb. Desperate the week before that when she'd called him four times in one day because she was sure the noise she was hearing outside her window could only be caused by an intruder.

"I've been calling you," Mrs. Winterberry said. "For ten minutes."

"I unplugged my phone." On purpose, he'd add, but that would offend her. And told her *she* was the reason he kept his phone disconnected when he worked.

He liked Mrs. Winterberry. She had that grand-motherly look about her, with her seemingly endless supply of cookies and muffins, and her mother-hen ways, but that package came equipped with a tendency to pop in unannounced, needing something almost every five minutes. When Dalton really needed to get this incredibly overdue book *done.*

"I'm sorry to bother you again, Dalton, but this time I really do need you. My sister…" Mrs. Winterberry's face flushed, and something churned in Dalton's gut, telling him this wasn't a lightbulb or a too-high can on Mrs. Winterberry's kitchen shelf, "my sister had a heart attack and…" She pressed a hand to her mouth. Her light blue eyes began to water.

Immediate regret flooded Dalton. He leapt to his feet, and crossed to the older woman, then stood there, helpless, not quite a friend, but not quite a stranger, either. In that next-door-neighbor-limbo of too distant to give a hug. Not that he was the hug type anyway. "I'm so sorry, Mrs. Winterberry. Ah, do you need a ride to the hospital?"

"No. But I do need you to…" She gave him a hopeful smile. "Watch Sabrina."

"Sabrina?"

Mrs. Winterberry made a vague wave toward the downstairs. "Yep. She's sleeping downstairs. All her things are there." Mrs. Winterberry started to leave.

"Wait. Who? What things?"

His neighbor poked her head back in. "I thought I told you. I've been looking after her for a neighbor. Ellie Miller? She lives in the little house across the street? You know, the brown one with the…"

Dalton looked back at his computer, not listening to the long-winded house description. Daylight was burning, as was his editor's short-fused temper. And he was no closer to being done. He had no time or desire to be watching so much as a neighbor's houseplant. "Mrs. Winterberry, isn't there another—"

"Don't worry," she interrupted, misinterpreting what he was about to say. "I left Ellie a message. She should be here any minute. Surely, you can watch Sabrina until then? Besides, it will probably be good for you. Give you a whole new perspective for your work." Satisfied his non-answer was a yes, Mrs. Winterberry headed for the door of his office and down the stairs, her mind clearly on her sister and not on anything else. "Thank you!"

Before he could say yes or no, Mrs. Winterberry

was gone. A second later, he heard the front door slam.

Dalton bit back a groan. Why had he ever shared the angst of a writer with his next-door neighbor? He'd been living alone too long, that was for sure. And now she'd left him with Sabrina, whoever that was. Probably the neighbor's cat. Mrs. Winterberry, self-proclaimed friend of the furry, was well-known for taking on people's pets when they went out of town.

Just great. Now he had a pooch or a cat to contend with. Well, it could be worse. He could be stuck with—

A piercing wail cut through the quiet of his house. No, it didn't *cut,* it viciously *slashed* the silence. "What the—?"

Dalton ran out of his office and into the massive, two-story great room, spinning, searching for the source of the sound. At first, in the huge space, he couldn't find the thing, praying it was a disc in his CD player, or someone outside, a screech of a teenager doing a one-eighty on the cul-de-sac, and then finally, his gaze lighted on a bundle of pink blankets squirming in a plastic rocker kind of thing on the floor by his favorite armchair.

A kid.

He crossed the room, moved the blankets to the side. And faced his worst nightmare. A baby.

Hell, no. Not a kid. He didn't do kids.

Ever.

Regardless, there was one. Kicking and screaming. And in his living room.

Its mouth was open in a cavernous O, the sound coming from its lungs reaching decibels usually reserved for deaf rock bands. Dalton was half tempted to put the blanket back, return to his office and shut the door. Except someone would eventually show up on his doorstep, demanding he do something about the human noisemaker. And besides, even he wasn't grumpy enough to leave a baby screaming in the middle of his living room.

"Hey," he said. "Hey!"

The baby kept screaming.

"Hey!" Dalton repeated, louder this time. "Cut it out. I'm not in the mood."

This time, the baby stopped. Looked at him. All blue eyes and red cheeks. A sliver of a memory raced through Dalton.

Damn.

He closed his eyes for a second, but that only made the past push its way out of the mental closet and into the forefront of Dalton's brain. He opened his eyes and let out a breath. It was better when the baby had been crying, loud enough to keep him from hearing himself think. He took three steps back, putting some distance between himself and the bundle of pink, and in the process, between his mind and those memories. They dissipated a little, but didn't disappear. Not entirely.

He needed to get this kid out of here. *That's* what he really needed to do.

Then he could work. Try to wrangle that manuscript back into something resembling readable, and at the same time get his career back in order.

"Listen, kid. I've got work to do. You can just sit there and be quiet. I'm going to see if Mrs. Winterberry is still here and tell her to find someone else. There's *no way* I can babysit." He wagged a finger in the infant's direction. "And I mean it. Not a peep out of you, understood?"

The baby blinked, grabbed the edge of her blanket with her fist. Probably scared into submission.

Good. Now he could concentrate again.

He headed for the front door. Hopefully, he could catch Mrs. Winterberry before she pulled out of her driveway. The elderly woman wasn't exactly a speed demon behind the wheel.

As soon as he was out of the kid's line of sight, the wailing began again. Apparently, someone didn't take direction well. Dalton opened the door anyway, stuck his head out, and saw—

No one. Not a soul. Mrs. Winterberry's driveway,

two doors away, was empty and silent, her familiar gray car gone.

Leaving him stuck.

He spun back toward the baby. "Stop. I mean it." He wagged a finger at the kid. A gurgle, a blink, and then a few sputters before she stopped.

He stared at her. She stared at him. Trusting. Almost… happy.

Damn. No way. He couldn't do this. He hadn't been around a baby since—

Well, he simply wasn't going to watch her. That's all there was to it.

The problem? He didn't see another available adult human option. He was "it" and he hadn't even asked to play tag.

Dalton crossed his arms over his chest. "So whose kid are you? Mrs. Winterberry said you belong to someone named…" He thought a second. What had she said? "Elsie? Emmie."

The kid was no help. There was no answer. Just some blinking. A blubbering lip.

"Don't start."

She whimpered, and threatened to let loose one more time. He shifted his weight and then did what he'd been hoping he wouldn't have to do—

He bent down and got close to the kid. There had to be a name tag or something on her. First, he inspected the car seat, bringing it forward and back, turning it right, left, sending the toys on the handle jingling and jangling. Hoping for an "If Lost, Return To" sticker.

Nothing.

He lifted the blankets, peeking underneath an inch at a time, wishing kids came equipped with a Paddington Bear tag. What was wrong with America? Really, all kids needed a stamp or GPS tracking or something so they could be sent back to whence they came.

But this one had nothing. And that meant Dalton was stuck with his worst nightmare and the one thing he, of all people, shouldn't be left in charge of.

A small child.

Ellie Miller's day had done nothing but get busier. Her best intentions had been derailed before she'd even arrived at work, given the number of e-mails and messages that had greeted her. Not to mention the meetings that had followed, one after another like dominoes. She let out a sigh and sank into the leather chair behind her desk, facing the inch-thick stack of pink message slips, accompanied by a furiously blinking phone. One two-hour meeting, and her afternoon had exploded in her absence.

If she wasn't stuck in meetings half the day—most of which were about as productive as trying to fill a hole-riddled bucket—she'd get much more done in a quarter of the time.

So much for her plan to leave early and spend the afternoon with Sabrina.

The tear in her heart widened. Every day, the ache between wishing she was home, and the need to be here at work, at a job she once thought she loved—but more, needed to keep to pay the bills, to keep her and Sabrina afloat, carved a deeper hole in her gut. How did other women do it? How did they balance the family and work worlds?

"One pink message slip at a time," Ellie muttered to herself and started flipping through the papers. As a producer for a newly launched celebrity interview TV show in the hot Boston market, downtime wasn't a word in her vocabulary. It wasn't a word she could afford, much less worry about.

Besides, she'd worked for years to reach this rung on the career ladder, to finally have a chance to prove herself capable. Okay, so it wasn't *exactly* what she'd gone to college for. This job was a bit of a detour from what she'd dreamed of while attending Suffolk University. Still, the television work would serve well on her résumé and could lead to what she really wanted down the road— or at least she kept telling herself that as she sat through another of Lincoln's pointless meetings.

Either way, she'd probably be destroying her career if she walked away now.

Ellie sighed. Not that her bank account could even entertain that option.

The pressure of being everything—mother, father, provider—weighed on her, more and more every day. Ellie tried to ignore it. She was a single mother. No amount of worry was going to change that situation. Even if sometimes she wondered whether she was handling the job very well.

Ellie glanced at Sabrina's picture, her heart clenching at the sight of her sweet eight-month-old, then she glanced back at the pile of missed messages. Work. A means to a better end.

Connie had marked the same checkbox on every one of the message slips: URGENT. Everything about this new job fit into that category, considering they'd hit the air a week ago. Finding guests, slotting stories—it all slammed into Ellie's days like a five-day-a-week hurricane.

At least a third of the messages had Mrs. Winterberry's name at the top. Ellie smiled and passed by those without reading them. She usually saved those for lunch, like a personal dessert, for when she had time to marvel over the details of Sabrina's day and call Mrs. Winterberry back. Mrs. Winterberry was a great babysitter—but one who thought she should call and report on every bottle feeding, every diaper change, every coo and gurgle.

Details that Ellie loved to hear—but that also made her miss her daughter more. If only *she* could be the one hearing those coos. Or be the one on the other end of those bottles. Every morning Ellie dropped off Bri—

And seemed to leave a part of her heart behind.

Regardless, Mrs. Winterberry had been a godsend. She watched Sabrina for a very reasonable fee—one much cheaper than any daycare in Boston would have charged. She'd seen the dire straits Ellie had been in, taken pity on her—and probably fallen in love with Sabrina's big blue eyes.

Who wouldn't? Sabrina, in Ellie's personal opinion, was the cutest baby in the entire world.

Ellie picked up the picture of her daughter and traced Bri's face. "I miss you, baby," she whispered. "I'm doing the best job I can."

Then she replaced the image on her desk, and got back to work. For now, Mrs. Winterberry's messages would have to wait. If Ellie got too distracted by thoughts of Sabrina, she'd never get anything done.

Instead, she returned the call of a celebrity guest who was having second thoughts about her appearance on the show. Something about "thigh confidence," Connie had noted.

A knock sounded on Ellie's door and Connie poked her head inside. "I see you got your messages. Surprised you're still here."

"Are you kidding me?" Ellie paused, waiting for the ring on the other end. "With this stack to return, I'll be lucky to leave before next year."

From out in the hall, she heard Lincoln calling her name. "Ellie! Meeting in fifteen! Be ready!"

Damn. She'd forgotten to prepare that list of potential closed captioning sponsors for Lincoln. Yet another thing to add to a day that already seemed impossible. She ran a hand through her hair and told herself she could do this.

Connie's brows knitted in confusion. "So, you're okay with what Mrs. Winterberry did?"

At the celebrity's office, a bored receptionist picked up. "Hi," Ellie said, "this is Ellie Miller, returning Julie Weston's call. Is she in?" The receptionist muttered something that could have been assent, then classical hold music filled the line. Ellie glanced back at Connie. "What did Mrs. Winterberry do now? Let me guess. Take Sabrina to the mall and spoil her mercilessly? I swear, that woman is a saint. She's bought more clothes for my daughter than I have."

"Yeah, well, read your message," Connie said, wagging a pen in the direction of Ellie's desk. "Babysitter-of-the-Month had to dump your kid and run. Her sister was sick or something. I couldn't really hear her. Lincoln was in the middle of a rant."

Just as Julie said hello, Ellie hung up on her and started rifling through the stack of messages again. Connie had organized them chronologically, and as Ellie flipped wildly, she saw the story take shape. "Mrs. Winterberry called. Needs you to call back. May need to leave early." "Mrs. Winterberry again. Sister is sick. Needs you to come home." "Mrs. Winterberry can't reach you. Leaving Sabrina with a neighbor."

A rising tide of worry flooded Ellie's chest. She ripped her cell phone out of her purse—still off from earlier, from the meeting, a Lincoln rule—never, ever interrupt a meeting with a phone call. Damn. At the same time she pressed the power button, Ellie pointed at the name below the word "neighbor" and glanced at Connie. "Neighbor? What neighbor?"

Ellie barely knew anyone in her neighborhood. She'd lived there just over a year and a half, and hadn't been outside to do much more than mow the lawn—and even that was sporadic. Her entire life was wrapped up in work, and Sabrina.

"Some guy named…uh, Dave or Dalton or something, I think. Again, Lincoln, screaming. Sorry. Lives uh…" Connie leaned forward, peering at her illegible words. "Across the street? At…529? Maybe 527? Sorry, El. The phone was ringing off the hook and that new voice mail is so spotty, people kept getting bounced back to me. Between that and Lincoln, I was having a heck of a time keeping up."

Ellie wanted to scream at Connie, to tell her that was no excuse for missing the details, but she had pitched in a time or two herself to work the front desk and knew how insane it could get. Plus, she didn't have time. Sabrina was with a stranger—and that had Ellie's heart racing. Her little girl was probably completely upset by the change in her environment, schedule, caretaker. Ellie could swear she heard Sabrina's cries from here. She shouldn't have gone to work today. She should have stayed home, stayed with Bri.

But that was an impossible dream. The job situation that Ellie had always wanted—but couldn't have.

She swung her purse over her shoulder and shoved away from her desk, clasping the last message in her hand. "I've got to go. Will you tell—"

"Lincoln," Connie finished, with a nod and a comforting touch on Ellie's arm. "I'll face the firing squad for you." She grinned. "Now, go."

"Thanks." Ellie was already out of her chair

and out the door, hurrying past Connie and down the stairs, bypassing the elevator to hustle down the three flights of stairs to the parking garage. Within minutes, she was in her car and on her way to her house, trying hard to concentrate on the road, not the fact that she didn't know this Dave/Dalton/whoever he was from a hole in the wall, and an hour had already passed since Mrs. Winterberry left the message. A thousand things could have gone wrong in that period of time.

But Mrs. Winterberry was responsible. Surely, she had left the neighbor babysitter with the list of numbers to reach Ellie. Mrs. Winterberry wouldn't have dumped her baby with just anyone.

Would she?

For the hundredth time since the death of her husband, Ellie wished she had a spouse to share this burden with, another parent to take on the emergencies. The late nights. The fretting over every detail.

At a stoplight, she dialed Mrs. Winterberry's cell phone number. "Mrs. Winterberry, thank God I reached you."

"Ellie! I'm so sorry I had to run out today. Don't you worry, Dalton Scott is a great babysitter. He comes from a family of twelve, you know. He's got *lots* of baby experience."

A whoosh of relief escaped Ellie. "Good."

"You didn't think I'd leave your baby with just anyone, did you?"

"Of course not."

Mrs. Winterberry laughed. "He's a very nice man, you know. A very nice man."

"I'm sure he is."

"He'd be nice for you. It's time you moved on, dear. Dealt with…well, dealt with losing your husband. I know, because I lost my Walter and it was the hardest thing I ever went through. You have a little one to think of. You need a man in your life, not just for you, but for that precious baby."

It was a familiar discussion. One Ellie had had a hundred times with her neighbor. But what Viola didn't understand was that moving on after Cameron's death involved a lot more than just dating a new guy. "Mrs. Winterberry, I don't have time—"

"No better time than now," she interrupted. "Well, dear. I have to get back to my sister. She's in rough shape but she'll be okay."

"Oh, Mrs. Winterberry. I'm so sorry."

"I probably have to stay a couple days. Maybe longer. I hate to leave you in a lurch, but—"

"Don't worry. Stay as long as you need. Take care of your sister. I'll be fine."

"Thank you, dear. I'll call you tomorrow. Give that little girl a kiss for me."

Ellie promised to do so, then hung up. She gripped the steering wheel and prayed for strength for the days ahead. Without Mrs. Winterberry's kindness, wisdom—and most importantly, her second set of hands—Ellie would be lost.

Stress doubled in Ellie's gut. She could tick the worries off, worries that had multiplied minute-by-minute in the months since she'd been widowed. Being a single mom. Paying the bills, the mortgage, a mortgage she'd taken on when there'd been two incomes, and been left to pay with one. Raising her child alone, juggling late-night feedings and diaper changes, while still managing to get to work, and be a star performer eight to ten hours a day. At the same time, the even-more-powerful desire to be a star mom. To give her all to her daughter, who needed her, and depended on her for everything. Every morning, Ellie woke up to trusting blue eyes that believed in Ellie to be a supermom, who could do it all.

And here, Ellie felt like she was barely balancing any of it.

Finally, she pulled onto her street. She parked haphazardly against the sidewalk opposite to her house, then paused outside the two houses. 527 or 529?

She should have asked Mrs. Winterberry. Damn. The crying answered the question for her. She could hear her daughter's cries through the open windows of 529, a massive two-story contemporary with a brick front she had noticed from time to time. A beautiful house, one of the nicest in the neighborhood. Ellie pressed the doorbell, then rapped on the oak door, resisting the urge to just barge in.

No answer. Sabrina kept crying.

Anxiety pattered in Ellie's chest. She rang the bell a second time, then knocked again, harder, more urgent this time. "Dalton? It's Ellie Miller. Mrs. Winterberry left Sabrina here, and I'm her—"

"Go away. I'm busy."

Sabrina cried louder.

Oh God. Was she hurt? What kind of guy was he? Despite Mrs. Winterberry's endorsement, he sounded grumpy. A horrible babysitter. Ellie turned the handle, said a silent prayer it would open, and—

It did.

Throwing Ellie into sheer chaos. Sabrina crying, squirming, in her car seat. The scent of a dirty diaper filling the room like it had exploded, and taken no prisoners in doing so. And at the far end of the room, one hand pinching his nose, the other holding aforementioned diaper in the manner usually reserved for toxic waste, a tall, dark-haired man with a scowl.

"What are you doing to my baby?"

From far across the room, he stepped on a trash

can pedal, tossed the diaper inside, then, once the can slammed shut, turned to her, his scowl deepening. "What am *I* doing? What is *she* doing is more like it. That kid should come with a condemned sign."

Ellie shot him a horrified glare, then hurried over to Sabrina, unclipping the safety belt before taking her out of the seat, and brought the baby to her chest. The scent of baby powder met Ellie's nostrils, sweet and pure. Ellie held her daughter tight, the warm, familiar body fitting perfectly into her arms. "Momma's here, sweetheart, Momma's here."

Having her child against Ellie felt like coming home. As if the world had been careening out of control all day, and suddenly everything had been righted again. Ellie let out a breath, her nerves no longer strung as tight as piano wire.

And every time, Ellie expected Bri to simply melt into her mother's touch, to calm gently. Coo and gurgle, like other babies. Be happy, content, like a commercial for motherhood, just like Ellie had dreamed during her pregnancy. But it never seemed to work that way.

As usual, Sabrina didn't calm down. She kept on crying, the volume rising, rather than lowering. Ellie did everything the books and Mrs. Winterberry had recommended. Rubbed Bri's back. Whispered in her ear. Started to pace. The baby, still worked up, continued to squirm and kick against Ellie's midsection. Clearly, being in the hands of another hadn't made Sabrina happy.

Ellie tried not to take the cries personally, but still…

She did.

"Come on, sweetie, it's okay."

Sabrina didn't agree. Her feet kicked. Her fists curled into tight circles. Her mouth opened and closed, letting out cry after cry. Ellie walked back and forth, circling the burgundy leather sofa, her high heels sinking into the plush carpet, creating a rippled path in Dalton's living room.

And still Sabrina didn't quiet. "Shh," Ellie soothed, nearly on the verge of tears herself. She tried so hard to be a good mother and still she had yet to connect, to get the baby to be happy. Was it because she was working too much? Because she came home too tired at the end of the day? Or was she simply a terrible mother? "Shh."

"Can't you get her to be quiet?" Dalton finished washing his hands, then exited the kitchen, tossing a dish towel over his shoulder and onto the counter as he did.

"What do you think I'm trying to do?" Ellie said, and kept pacing.

"By the way, even though I've seen you across

the street, I don't believe we've been formally introduced. I'm Dalton Scott," he said, extending a hand. "Reluctant temporary babysitter."

Ellie shifted Sabrina to the opposite shoulder, hoping that would help. It didn't. "Ellie Miller. Thanks for watching her." She let out a gust. "I apologize for being hard on you earlier. I know how difficult it can be to balance a million things at once, especially with an eight-month-old. The diapers, the crying. It can get to the best of us, even me."

"Yeah. Well, don't ask me to do it again." He gestured toward the baby with his head. "Unless you send earplugs."

"Sorry. She's not usually this difficult." Well, maybe not for other people. Either way, Ellie wasn't telling the truth and showing herself to be Completely Awful Mom of the Year. Ellie again changed Sabrina's position, but if anything that made the cries intensify. Ellie drew in a breath, trying to work up some more patience into a day that had already been extra frustrating. "Come on, baby, calm down. Okay?" Sabrina kept on crying, nearly squirming out of Ellie's arms.

"Hey, you," Dalton said, putting his face in near to Sabrina's, his voice low, stern. No-nonsense. Ellie turned her focus away from him, trying not to notice the intensity of his blue eyes, the deep waves of his dark hair. The muted notes of his cologne. He said it again, a third time, each time waiting for a break in the baby's cries. "Cut that out."

Sabrina turned and looked at him. Then, to Ellie's surprise, she snarfled, then paused, her chest still heaving, like she was about to burst into tears again. But didn't.

"That's right. We talked about this, didn't we?" he went on. "None of that—not in my house."

Ellie stared at him. A feeling of hurt filled her chest. He had done what she, as Sabrina's mother, had not been able to do. In seconds. With a few words. And here she'd practically stood on her head, and gotten nowhere.

She was Bri's *mother,* she was supposed to have a natural touch with her own baby. And here came this guy, a *total stranger,* who presto-whammo, calmed Bri with a few words and a *look?*

What did that say about Ellie? Had it gotten to the point where Sabrina was closer to her sitters than her own mother?

Was this the price she paid for working too much?

"You got her to stop crying," Ellie said.

"I didn't *get* her to do anything. I just told her to quit." He scowled again—Ellie didn't think the man had another facial gesture—and turned away. "Now that she has, you both can get out of my hair. And I can get back to work."

Then he turned on his heel, and marched up the stairs. A second later, a door slammed upstairs.

Ellie's jaw dropped. How rude.

She didn't need his attitude, and Sabrina definitely didn't need to be around such a disagreeable human being. Ellie grabbed the car seat and started to reach for the diaper bag. Then she stopped.

Where was she going to go? Back to work, Sabrina in tow?

That would never work. She'd tried that—once—when Mrs. Winterberry had been sick, and it had been a disaster. Sabrina was like any baby—needy and demanding—and bringing her into the chaotic, busy environment of Revved Up Productions just added to the office zoo. Lincoln, the epitome of stress, had become even more stressed, and nearly fired her on the spot. And now that Sabrina was starting to crawl, taking her to work would be an epic disaster.

Working at home didn't fare much better. Every time a call came in, Sabrina would inevitably need a bottle, a diaper change or rocking at the same time. A screaming baby and a phone call—not a good mix.

Every day, Ellie was forced to make a choice, and inevitably, Sabrina was the loser, because in the end, what had to come first was paying for the roof over their heads, a roof she could barely afford on her own. She'd been trying so hard, and feeling like she'd failed every day. And now—

What was she going to do?

Lose her job?

Reality slammed into Ellie. Mrs. Winterberry wouldn't be back for several days, at least. Ellie had no back-up plan—she'd had no time, in fact, to put one in place, and kept thinking tomorrow, tomorrow she'd find another sitter who could fill in if something like this arose.

Now that someday was here and Ellie was thrown into chaos. With Sabrina caught in the middle of the storm. Ellie buried her face in the sweet scent of that innocent, trusting face, a face that believed Ellie would do the right thing, would always keep the world on an even, perfect keel.

And once again, Ellie was alone, desperately navigating a rushing river with an oar-less boat.

How was she going to manage this? She clutched Sabrina tighter, trying to hold on to her emotions, her life, her sanity—and suddenly it all got away from her, escaping in a gush of tears as she realized Mrs. Winterberry's absence meant one thing.

If Ellie Miller didn't find a miracle in the next five minutes, she'd lose her job. And in the process, lose everything that mattered to her.

CHAPTER TWO

"WHAT the hell do you think you're doing?"

Dalton stared at the woman and her kid, standing in his sacred space. He'd stalked up to his office, figuring they would find their own way back out the front door. After all, she'd let herself in, she could damned well let herself out. But no, she'd gone and followed him.

"You…you can't walk away…I need help."

And worse, she was crying.

"*I* need to work. And *you* need to go home." He turned back to his computer. Pretended he didn't see the tears. But they bothered him all the same. If there was one thing Dalton Scott couldn't take, it was tears.

He stood in front of his desk for the second time that day as helpless as a fish on dry land, while Ellie Miller held her baby and cried.

"You're right. This is my problem, not yours."

"Exactly." He sat down in his chair. Pulled his keyboard closer.

She didn't leave. He could tell. Because he could still hear her crying.

"It's just…"

He let out a long sigh and turned around. "Just what?"

"I…" She bit her lip. "I don't know what else to do."

"Hire a babysitter."

"I did. She's not here."

"Hire another one." He turned back to his computer. Looked at the words on the screen. They were all horrible. Every last one of them. Dalton started hitting the backspace key. In the last hour, this book had multiplied badness.

"It's not that easy."

She was still here? He spun back toward the woman and her kid. "I'm trying to work here."

Aw, damn, the tears were really pouring down her face. They'd made rivers on her cheeks. Even the kid was staring at him, as if saying *what are you going to do about this?*

Well, he knew what he *wasn't* going to do. He wasn't going to let them stay here, in his office. This was his domain, and already Mrs. Winterberry had been here, disrupting his train of thought. He had enough problems writing, without adding these two into the mix.

"Let's go back downstairs," he said, practically shooing them out the door. "Get a cup of coffee or something."

Why did he have to add that? His goal was to get them out the door, not serve hot beverages.

A moment later, though, the woman and her kid were in his living room. She lowered herself onto the leather seat, a whisper of relief flickering across her delicate features. She dropped the car seat to the floor, and propped the kid on her lap, holding the baby tight against her chest. Together, they looked like bedraggled street orphans. Dalton almost—almost—felt his heart going out to them.

Well, just for that he wouldn't make any coffee. He dropped into the opposite armchair, watching the tears continue to stream down her face, still feeling about as comfortable as a porcupine in a roomful of balloons. He handed her a box of tissues from the endtable. "Here."

"Thanks."

"You're welcome."

She paused, and then her big green eyes met his, watery lakes filled with an ocean of thoughts.

"Are you better now?"

"Yeah."

"You don't seem it." Man, he could have just let

it go at her "yes," but he seemed to have this over-whelming compunction to *get involved* today.

She glanced down at the tissue, clasped in front of her. "I can't go back to work, not with Sabrina. And I can't go home, because I can't afford to call in sick until Mrs. Winterberry comes back. I'm barely paying my bills as it is. Without Mrs. Winterberry, I'm stuck and I don't know what I'm going to do…" She started crying again, the tears falling in a slow stream, disappearing into the fuzz on her daughter's head.

Did he have a "please pull at my heartstrings, I'll help anyone today" sign in his front yard or something?

As much as Dalton wanted to tell her "too bad, lady, you're on your own," he couldn't get the words out, not when he saw those tears, the slump in her shoulders, the despair on her face. He cleared his throat. "What you need is…"

Ellie looked up.

"Someone to watch the kid."

"You would do that?" The hope that filled her face blossomed like a sunflower.

"I never said…"

"It would only be for a day or two."

He put his hands up. "Lady, I have a job here. And it's not going so well lately. Kids are an interruption—"

"I know, I know. I've tried working at home with her and it was so hard."

Aw, that hope in her voice. He wanted to counteract it. Yell at her. Tell her he had his life just the way he liked it, thank you very much and get out of my house, but she was looking at him like he was her savior, and when he opened his mouth to say *go home, find another option*—

He couldn't do it.

"Really, you'd be helping me so much. I can't even begin to—"

"Then don't," he interrupted. If she started to thank him one more time, he'd tell her no. He hadn't even agreed to watching her kid, had he? No. He was going to tell her to find someone else. Yes. That's what he'd do. He had a book to finish. A career to salvage. He didn't need a baby underfoot, and he'd tell her so. Right now. "*If* I watched your kid for a couple days it would be a complete in—"

She sprang out of the chair and crossed to him, as if she might hug him. "Oh, thank you! You saved—"

"Will you stop thanking me?"

What the hell did he just do? And worse, what did he just *say?*

Oh, he was stuck now. She already assumed he was going to watch the kid. What was he going to do? Tell her no? And start the waterworks up again?

Quickly, he turned and headed toward his kitchen, away from this new burst of emotion, and most of all, the potential for a hug from her and the kid. She'd taken his words and assumed he said yes and now he was in a mess. A mess of his own making.

From his own stupid words. Apparently, his lack of writing ability extended to his verbal ability, too.

"I'm going to make some lunch," he called over his shoulder. "You, ah, want some?"

It was a lame change of subject. An escape, really. But suddenly he'd had to get away from those eyes, from that burst of joy on her face. It had been so powerful, so…

Trusting.

As if she'd just put her whole world in his palms.

She had no idea what she was doing. And he should have thought before he'd opened his big, idiot mouth.

He didn't want a kid in his house. Definitely didn't need a kid in his house. He'd almost had this one *out* the door and here he'd accidentally invited it to stay for a couple of days by not saying what he'd meant to say fast enough. And all because she'd started crying. He was definitely getting soft. Maybe if he got in the kitchen, he could make her a ham sandwich and in the meantime, come up with a way to get out of this deal. A way to soften the blow of saying, *hey, I changed my mind. Find another neighbor.*

Clearly not reading his mind—or his need for space—Ellie trotted right along behind him and into the kitchen, the kid in her arms. "I'm so glad you offered to watch her. I really am desperate. My job is—"

"I don't need to hear the details." He opened the fridge, ducked his head inside, trying to head off further personal information.

She was a hard woman to ignore, and not just because she kept on following him. Dalton had no idea how he had missed this particular neighbor. Well, being a hermit for the last three months didn't help, but still, he had to have been blind not to notice this curvy brunette, with her vivid green eyes and full crimson mouth.

A mouth that wouldn't quit bugging him.

"I'm a producer for a new TV show for Channel 77, and the demands on my time right now are incredible. Missing a day of work is out of the question. In fact—" she flung out her wrist and looked at her watch "—I need to get out of here before my boss has a coronary. But before I go, I really want to ask a few more questions. An interview, of sorts."

"*Now* you want to interview me? I already

watched your kid. She came back to you intact, fed, and clean, didn't she?"

Ellie ignored that credential. "What do you do for a living? Are you available from eight to six every day? If this is going to interfere with your job, I'll need to make some arrangements."

He leaned against the counter and crossed his arms over his chest. "I'm a writer. I work here. It's a pretty flexible job."

The kid perked up in the woman's arms. Apparently, the job impressed the under-one-year-old set.

"You must be doing pretty well. I mean, you have a really nice house."

He scowled. "Maybe I have a wealthy patron to support me." She didn't need to know how he'd started out as a successful writer, hitting the top of the charts, then slammed into a major block and plummeted to the bottom. Or how he'd spent the last year struggling to whip this latest opus into an acceptable form. How he'd sweated over every word, every page, and still ended up ripping out seventy percent of what he'd written. Because this book, just like the last few, was lacking the one element his editor had been on his back to add—

Emotion.

She smiled. "Will you still be able to balance your writing with watching my daughter? I don't want to take away from your work." She shifted the baby, who was watching him as intently as a puppy hoping to get lucky with a crumb. What was it with this kid? He seemed to have some kind of mesmerizing effect on it.

Must be the stranger thing. She didn't know him, ergo, she just stared. Like he was a shiny new toy.

"I'm…stuck right now. I have time to watch a kid." No, he wanted to scream at himself. He did not have time to watch a kid. But then again, this woman did need help. And it hadn't been *so* awful this morning. Maybe he could suck it up for a few more hours, until she found some other neighbor to take on her and her baby. If he was lucky, the kid would nap the whole time.

"Stuck?" Her brows lifted in a question. "What do you mean?"

He pushed off from the counter and took a step closer to her. "Listen, this isn't about my book writing skills. I offered to help you out and watch your kid. That's all."

Okay, Dalton. So much for saying you changed your mind.

"You're right," she said. "It's just, as a new mother, I tend to get pretty overprotective, which means I also get really personal. So I'm sorry if I asked too many questions. I just want to make sure that if she cries or needs something, you'll be there."

"Beck and call guy, that's me." The words were meant to reassure Ellie, but in the back of his head, he wondered what he was getting himself into. Taking care of a baby all day?

Him?

He had his life just the way he liked it. Alone, and quiet. He didn't need a kid around.

But this woman clearly needed someone to help her out—and it wouldn't kill him to be a nice guy for twenty-four hours. Would it?

Ellie shifted the baby to the other hip. The kid protested the move with a series of cries. Ellie rubbed her back, peppered kisses across her forehead, and Sabrina quieted. She laid her head on Ellie's shoulder, her eyes beginning to shut. A surge of something Dalton refused to name rose in his chest—a feeling from long ago, one he'd pushed away.

At the same time, Ellie's cell phone began to ring. She dug it out of her pocket, let out a gust, muted the phone, then stuffed it back. As soon as she did, it started ringing again, which made the baby give up on the sleeping thing. Ellie brushed her bangs out of her face, then fished the phone out one more time and answered it. "Hi, Lincoln," she said, continuing to rub the kid's back with the other hand—making the whole balancing act look way too complicated to Dalton. The baby started to whine, so Ellie tried a pacifier that was attached to the kid by a clip and a ribbon, but the kid spat it back. Ellie returned to the back rub, but this time, the circular motion's magic failed. "Yes, I'm on my way. Of course I have available child care. I just had to stop by for a—" She paused. "I know, I know this meeting's important. Wouldn't miss it for the world. I'll be—" An embarrassed smile took over her face. "He hung up. He's a little tense."

Lincoln. A boyfriend? Boss?

Husband?

The kid voiced a protest, as if she understood what the cell phone's ring meant.

Ellie held out the baby toward Dalton. "I have to go. Thank you again."

"You're leaving? *Already?*" Now that the moment was here, panic gripped him. She was leaving him with the kid? Now? Why had he made this offer? What had he been thinking?

"Is that a problem? I thought you just said you could watch Sabrina."

"Yeah, well I hadn't expected you to be leaving so soon." He glanced at the clock. Only eleven in the morning. Six o'clock seemed like eons away.

"Believe me, I wish I didn't have to leave," she said, bringing the baby back to her chest and holding her tight again. "If I could take Bri with me, or find a different way to work and still be with her…" Her voice trailed off and she let out a sigh. "But I can't." Ellie gave the kid another bunch of kisses, and this time whispered something nonsensical against her skin.

Dalton swallowed hard. "You should go," he said, even though he wanted her to stay. He simply couldn't watch that look on her face for one more second.

It opened up way too many doors he'd thought he'd firmly shut a long time ago.

"You're right, I need to go. One more thing. If anything happens to Sabrina," she said quietly, a mother bear growl deep in her voice, "I'll sue you for everything you're worth, and throw you into jail until you're a hundred and ten."

"I thought you trusted me."

She looked up from her kid's head. "I *need* you. I don't *trust* you. I don't trust anyone. Sabrina is all I've got and—" Her phone started up again. Ellie rolled her eyes, then flipped it open. "On my way, I swear." The phone went back in her pocket, and was exchanged for a business card. "My cell phone number is on there, as is my office phone. Call me every half hour and give me an update."

"Update on what? If she burped?"

"Yes."

"You're kidding me. Kids do nothing all day.

They eat, they poop, they sleep. There. That's your update."

Her jaw dropped in horror. He expected her to tell him off, but instead she turned away. A second later her shoulders were heaving and then, she was doing it again—

Crying.

Well, not exactly crying, more, holding her kid and looking like she might let loose with the waterworks at any second. Damn. He hadn't been around this much estrogen since he lived at home.

He stood behind Ellie, his hands at his sides, useless and awkward. His chest constricted, lungs caught. A part of him said to reach out and hug her.

The other part said not to get involved. He listened to that part, deciding it was the side with more sense.

She nuzzled at the kid's head, as if she was breathing in her hair. Dalton focused his gaze on the name branded across his refrigerator and avoided the private moment as best he could. Except it was right there in his kitchen. Inescapable.

"I hate leaving you. I hate it," she said, more to herself than the baby, her voice nearly a whisper.

"Then quit," Dalton suggested. Ever Mr. Helpful.

"I can't. I have to pay the bills."

"Then quit complaining."

She wheeled around. "You are the most unsympathetic man—"

"I'm not unsympathetic. I'm matter-of-fact. The way I see it, you have two choices. Quit, or buck up." Half of him said he should reach out, swipe away the tears on her face, and a small part of him ached to do just that. But he didn't know her and she'd probably deck him if he touched her. "Moaning about it isn't going to get you anywhere."

"I just had a baby. I'm…hormonal. You could be a little understanding."

"*I'm* being logical."

"You probably think I'm a basket case. All I've done is cry today. It's just…" She drew in a breath, let it out again. "I've got a lot going on personally and I've had a really bad day at work, and then, with this whole Mrs. Winterberry thing and seeing you with her, it brought up every emotion I try to keep bottled up."

He didn't know what to say to that. So he didn't say anything.

"Every time I'm at work, I miss Sabrina like crazy. I'm like any new mom, I guess. You practically have to pry her out of my arms." Her face softened, nearly melting with love and the kind of heartbreak that told him a part of her gut wrenched in half when she left her kid behind every morning.

Dalton might not be the nicest guy in Boston,

but even he could see this was hard on her. Where was her husband? And why wasn't he stepping up to share the burden? Either way, it wasn't Dalton's place to get involved, at least not beyond this temporary babysitting thing.

"I do have a crowbar in the garage, and I'm not afraid to use it," he teased, tossing Ellie a grin, waiting until she echoed the smile, and when she did, it was as if a ray of sunshine had burst right there in his living room.

It hit him in the gut. Hard. Before he could think about how that felt, he stepped forward, figuring he better take the lead or she'd be working her way through another box of tissues on him. He took the kid out of her arms, holding the baby gingerly, like she was a sack of C-4 explosives, keeping her from too much direct contact.

"Now get to work," he said to Ellie, his tone gentler than he'd ever heard it, surprising even him. "And hurry back." He gestured toward the door. "Because I don't do overtime."

Ellie's mind should have been on the guest sitting across from her. A three-time soccer champ, lauded the world over, not for his skills, but for his ability to woo women and rugged good looks that had propelled him—and his soccer ball—into the realm of teenage girl fantasies, splashing his mug across every under-eighteen-year-old's wall around the country.

But Ellie couldn't concentrate on the young athlete. Instead, she kept thinking about a certain irascible dark-haired, blue-eyed writer. She couldn't imagine him cooing to and spoiling Sabrina the way Mrs. Winterberry did, but she didn't think he'd neglect her or anything. He'd be efficient. As he called it, matter-of-fact. And for some reason, Sabrina seemed to take to him.

Find him fascinating.

It was something about his eyes.

The deep blue of them, perhaps. The way they tossed and turned, like an uneasy ocean. Sabrina certainly didn't notice all those details.

But Ellie did.

Noticed them in a visceral way that she hadn't noticed about a man in a long, long time.

Not since Cameron. Ellie closed her eyes and rubbed her temples. She'd vowed to move on with her life, to put the past where it should be—in the past. To not feel guilty because Cameron had told her to move on, to live her life.

To find someone else. A husband for herself. A father for Sabrina. Because he wouldn't be here to do the job himself.

"You're sure the lighting will be on my good side?" Barry Perkins asked. He took a comb out of his pocket, perfected already perfect blond hair, then flashed her a gleaming smile. "Because my fans will expect that, of course."

"Of course." Vanity, thy name is Barry Perkins. Ellie glanced down at her notepad, to jot a note about "good side," then felt her face heat. Instead of finding notes about the soccer player, her pad was covered with doodles of the letter "D."

She had Dalton on the mind. Not a good thing. Especially because the man annoyed her to the -nth degree. How anyone could be so grumpy, she had no idea. It certainly explained why she'd never seen him before. He defined the word "hermit."

She glanced at the picture of Sabrina on her desk. Was he holding Sabrina right now? Was her daughter laughing? Or crying? Or sleeping peacefully? Ellie's gaze darted to the phone, and she had to curl her fist tight around her pen to resist the urge to call Dalton and check up on the baby.

"You'll have filtered water in my dressing room, right? Along with dark chocolates, with raspberry centers? Make sure there aren't any strawberry or, God help me—" he pressed a hand to his forehead "—any coconut ones. Raspberry only."

Ellie forced a patient smile to her face. "Certainly."

Scheduling bottled waters and personalized

chocolates for male divas wasn't the life she had envisioned when she'd found out she was pregnant, and getting used to it had been a hundred times harder than Ellie had expected. She hadn't, in fact, expected to be working at all for the first year or two after Sabrina had been born. Cameron was supposed to be the breadwinner. She was supposed to be able to stay home with Bri, put her career on a temporary hold, and then get back into the swing of things.

Then Cameron had died, and Ellie had been thrust into the role of breadwinner, dual parent, homeowner, everything, all at once. The plan had gone horribly awry, and when she was here at her office at Channel 77, she simply couldn't think about Sabrina, because when she thought about all she was missing, it drove her insane.

And down the road, the thought of not seeing those first teeth, first steps, first words—

Forget it. Ellie was either going to have to hook up full-time video surveillance or find some kind of work-at-home job. The separation would surely kill her otherwise.

"I'll have my manager fax a list of my other requirements." The soccer player rose, then straightened his shirt, smoothing out invisible wrinkles. "I look forward to being the featured guest on your show."

If Ellie told him he was a five-minute segment following a former President, the soccer star would undoubtedly bolt—along with his supply of raspberry chocolates. He'd probably throw a major temper tantrum, which would take time Ellie didn't have. She wanted to get out of here on time—so she could get back to Sabrina. And if she was lucky, Lincoln would keep his afternoon golf date with the head of the TV station, and Ellie might even be able to sneak out early.

So instead she worked up another smile, shook the soccer player's hand, and walked him to the door. As soon as he left, and the female buzz in the office had died to manageable decibels, Ellie picked up her office phone and dialed Dalton's house.

So much for keeping her focus on her job. Maybe that video surveillance thing wasn't such a far-fetched idea after all.

"Hello?" He answered on the third ring. Barked, really.

"It's Ellie. Ellie Miller. You're watching my daughter?"

"You think I have so many kids over here I'd confused over which one belongs to who?"

"You *are* watching my daughter, aren't you?"

"Not really."

"What?"

"Calm down. She's sleeping. That does not

require me to stare at her, watching each and every breath."

Ellie wanted to argue back that it darn well did, but she knew better. Even she didn't watch every one of Sabrina's breaths, though there had been many times when Sabrina had been first born, especially in those last few precious days of maternity leave, that she had noted every blink, every movement, wanting to commit every second to memory. Even now, she felt as if she was missing so many millions of moments, ones she'd never be able to recoup. The familiar ache deepened. The walls closed in around her. The room had never felt more like a cage. "Then what are you doing?"

"Do you want all the details? Including any bathroom breaks? Or just the overall minute-by-minute?"

"Just the overall."

"She ate. I changed her diaper. She fell asleep. After she crawled all over my house. You should have warned me."

"Warned you?"

"Yeah, that the kid moves. I didn't know she was mobile. It was like following the Road Runner."

"I missed the first time she crawled," Ellie said softly. "Mrs. Winterberry called me and described every second of it. But it wasn't the same."

"Oh." Dalton paused a second. "Sorry to hear

that. Well, she crawled around a lot. Got her knees all dirty. Guess I need to get my cleaning lady in here more."

"Then what?"

He thought a second. "Then she fell asleep. So I went to work. You called. *Interrupted* my work. Now, can I get back to—"

"Did you burp her? Rock her? Make sure she has her pacifier? And her special blanket? If she wakes up and doesn't have those things, she'll get upset." Worry crowded Ellie's shoulders. She should never have left Sabrina with Dalton. He didn't know her daughter. Sabrina's likes and dislikes. How she preferred to sleep, with her blanket tucked under one arm, her pacifier nearby, but not in her mouth. Her favorite toy always around when she was on the floor—a vinyl mouse that squeaked when Sabrina squeezed it.

What if the baby got upset? Missed her mother? There were a million details to watch, and if Dalton missed one, Sabrina would cry, and the guilt would just kill Ellie.

Ellie should be there. "When was the last time you checked on her? Made sure she was okay?"

"Boy, you are tense, aren't you? I've been around kids before. She'll be fine."

But something wavered in his voice, and doubt rocketed through Ellie's gut. Mrs. Winterberry had assured her Dalton had plenty of experience with children.

Then why did he sound unsure? As if he doubted he'd know what to do, should his stare-into-her-eyes technique fail?

Had Ellie asked enough questions? Had she interviewed him thoroughly? Or left too fast this afternoon?

"Are you positive you don't want me to—"

"Ellie," Lincoln said, popping his head into her office, "meeting in three minutes."

"Dalton, can I call you back in a second?" When he agreed, she hung up and turned her attention to her boss. "I'll be there, Lincoln."

"Good. And bring your notes about the soccer diva-dude. We have to re-hash this morning's meetings. Seems no one got a clear picture of what I wanted. We need another run-through of the whole show." He ran a hand through his thick shock of white hair. A tall man given to loud suits, Lincoln had this perpetual look of stress about him, no matter what he did or what time of day it was. "Maybe you can get through to everyone. And translate my gobbledy-gook into something the rest of those morons will understand. I tell you, it's like working with a bunch of monkeys around here."

Ellie was tempted to tell Lincoln it was less

about morons, and more about his insistence on keeping his staff caged in the conference room for one unproductive hour after another. "Lincoln, maybe if you didn't have so many meetings…"

"Ellie, meetings are essential. They're where all the best ideas are born. Or they would be, if I actually employed people who possessed the brain cells to foster ideas. That's why I need you, Ellie. You're my right-hand woman. I swear, I couldn't function around here without you."

"You don't need seven hundred meetings a week to function, Linc."

He shook his head, refusing to have this argument. He started to walk away, then returned. "Oh, and Ellie, before I leave today, I wanted to tell you, I need you to create a script this afternoon. I need it on my desk first thing tomorrow."

"Create a script? Today?"

"Yeah. You know that celebrity chef, the one with the new book? Apparently he can't do anything but cook and read. So I need you to write him up something that makes him look and sound intelligent and entertaining." Lincoln smiled. "I know you can do it, Ellie. You're my can-do person. Let's have this meeting, then."

Ellie laid her head on her desk. So much for her plan to knock off early. Even if Lincoln wasn't here to oversee her, she had enough work to fill the entire rest of the day.

Every time she thought she'd get some time for herself…

It evaporated like rainwater on hot summer pavement. How she hated this job. But if she quit, how would she support Bri? Where else would she work? Any other job in television would be just as demanding. Ellie sighed, then reached for the phone and called Dalton back.

When he answered, the first thing she heard was Sabrina's loud wails, cutting through the phone lines like razors. Ellie's pulse quickened, mother's instinct beating inside her, telling her to go to her child—

"Is everything okay?"

"It's fine. She's crying. I gotta go."

"No, wait. Is she wet? Does she need to eat?"

Dalton let out an exasperated breath. "I don't know yet. That's why I'm trying to get off the phone and find out. Now are you going to let me go do that or not?"

Let Dalton hold Sabrina, let Dalton calm her down. The jobs *she,* as Sabrina's mother, should be doing—instead of heading in for yet another stupid, aimless meeting.

Did she have a choice? Lincoln trusted her to come up with something fabulous in the next three minutes. And right now, on her legal pad, her idea of fabulous looked a lot like letter D's.

"Wait," she said before Dalton could hang up.

Another exasperated gust. "What? Kid crying here, you know."

The knot of growing tension in her gut told her this arrangement with Dalton couldn't work. Her, sitting here, miles away from Sabrina. Missing her baby more and more every day, missing the scent of her, the feel of her in her arms, a pain that refused to stop. Her mind concocting ten thousand different possible scenarios of Dalton falling asleep, leaving the stove on, forgetting Sabrina at the park—

"I have an idea," Ellie said, knowing even as she said the words that there was no way she could make this work—and no way she could afford *not* to make it work, at least, for her heart. Money-wise, it was another story. "And I promise, you're going to love it."

"That's what my mother told me when she signed me up for ballroom dancing lessons when I was ten," Dalton said. "And I can tell you from personal experience that 'I have an idea' and 'you'll love it' doesn't always go together in my book."

CHAPTER THREE

BY THE time Ellie showed up on his doorstep, Dalton had thrown in the towel, raised the white flag, and tossed up his hands in surrender. The kid—who had originally been calmed with a stare—now wanted him to do the one thing he'd vowed not to do.

To be held.

He would feed her, change her diaper. Lay her down for a nap. Pick her up *momentarily,* basically just long enough to unload her again on the floor or into the car seat.

But walk around with the kid on his shoulder? No. Not part of the job description. And not something he, of all people, should be doing. For one, he had a childhood history of butterfingers with babies. His mother hadn't nicknamed him Dropsy Dalton for nothing. For another, he and babies didn't...bond well.

But there was more to it than that. Much more. A history Dalton didn't like to think about—

And wouldn't.

This was a temporary gig, one he'd taken on in a moment of clear emotional weakness, which meant he wasn't about to try to change that pattern. And he didn't have to. Before he knew it, he'd be done with the whole thing.

He was sitting in his armchair, pushing at Sabrina's car seat with his toe, rocking her back and forth. She had the plug in her mouth, but she was still managing to cry around it. Dalton was praying in his head for Sabrina to just give up the battle and go back to sleep.

Then his doorbell rang, and he heard knocking. "Dalton? It's Ellie."

Salvation had arrived.

He pulled open the door and let her in. "Finally. You're here. She's missed you." Actually, *he'd* probably missed Ellie more—strictly in a take-back-this-kid sense, of course.

A smile took over Ellie's face. The kind that socked Dalton in the gut and hit him with an almost envious feeling. Had anyone ever looked at him like that? Ever been that happy to see him at the end of the day? "I can hear that." She brushed past Dalton, beelined for the car seat, unsnapped the kid, and picked her up. A second later, she had the kid against her chest, working the circles again, and had quieted her down. Somewhat.

"You all set? If so, I'll go back to work." He handed Ellie the diaper bag, practically throwing it onto her shoulder.

"Wait. You haven't even heard my idea. Remember? I mentioned it to you on the phone?"

"Tell me later." He started toward his office. "You're here. My shift is over." Okay, so it was only three in the afternoon, probably too early for his shift—if that's what he could call it—to be anywhere near over, but Ellie was here, and that was good enough for him.

He was done. D-O-N-E. And not a moment too soon. What had he been thinking? Trying to take on a baby, of all things? He couldn't do this. *Shouldn't* do this.

All day, he'd tried to tell himself he could keep his distance. Not be taken in by those baby blue eyes and that gummy smile. That being with this kid wouldn't open up those doors he'd worked so hard to shut. Or disrupt his life.

He'd been wrong.

Now he wanted out. Away. And as fast as possible.

Dalton stalked off, heading straight upstairs, but Ellie followed behind, heck, acting as if she lived here. Right into his office. Again.

"Technically, you're not done yet. I still need a sitter because I'm still working. I've just changed…locations."

For the first time since she'd arrived, he noticed the thick leather bag hanging from her opposite shoulder. Papers bulged from every pocket. His gaze narrowed. "What do you mean, changed locations?"

"I had to get out of there. My boss was driving me crazy. But worrying about Bri was driving me more insane. And when my boss left for a golf game, I realized I could leave early, without anyone missing me today, so I thought maybe—"

His gaze narrowed. "Maybe what?"

"Maybe I could spend the rest of the day here. With you and Sabrina."

"With me. And the baby." The words weren't a question.

"I still have some work to do, and I'm sure you want to get some writing done, so I thought we could work together. That's the best of both worlds, don't you think?" She smiled. "Win-win."

"With you. And her here."

"You mentioned you've been stuck with your writing, right? Some kind of writer's block? Maybe having some company will give you some inspiration."

He put his back to his desk. To the fat pile of nothing stacked up beside his computer. "This is all because you really don't trust me, isn't it?"

"It's not that. It's…" The baby let out a whimper, and almost like an instinct, Ellie's body began to sway, her hips moving in this easy fashion, as if she had some kind of innate knowledge Dalton didn't possess.

He couldn't take his eyes off her. The movement was so natural, so feminine. And it stirred something deep inside him, something almost primal.

Dalton swallowed hard. He'd thought he could do this. Thought he could spend a few days with the kid, help out a woman in need, while also taking his mind off the fact that his book wasn't going so well.

But he couldn't.

"This won't work." He walked out of the office and headed downstairs again, back into the living room—Ellie still following like a determined puppy. He circled the room, gathering up the plethora of stuff the kid had—it looked like a baby explosion in his house—and started dumping it into the car seat. He hoisted the loaded car seat and held it out to Ellie. She ignored the pink and white kid container. "I'm…busy. And this is an interruption I don't need."

She turned and paced, thinking, her hips still in hula mode, while the kid kept fussing. Ellie worked the pacifier against the kid's mouth. "What are you writing?"

He drew up short, surprised by the abrupt shift in conversation. "What does that have to do with anything?"

"I'm just wondering."

"I write crime fiction. Thrillers. You know, catch the bad guy and all that."

She picked up one of his books from the end table and flipped it over. "Wow. Is that you?" She pointed to a publicity shot from several years ago.

"Yeah."

"You're not bad looking."

"Yeah. It's amazing what a good photographer and a graphic designer with some Photoshop experience can do."

She laughed. "Oh, I didn't mean that." She tapped the book. "You really are a good-looking man."

He'd been complimented by women before, but this woman—a determined spitfire if he'd ever seen one—well he sure hadn't expected her to say anything nice to or about him. The words left him a little discomfited, something Dalton rarely, if ever experienced. "Uh, thanks."

Ellie turned a few pages in the book. "These are really, really bad guys."

"Yeah."

She shook her head. "No wonder."

"No wonder what?"

"No wonder you're so grumpy. You spend your entire day cooped up with the worst the world has to offer."

"I'm not cooped up."

She arched a brow, then leaned forward. "When was the last time you went to the park?"

"Park? What park?"

"The one around the corner, at the end of Elm, silly." She laughed at his blank look. "You *really* need to get out more."

"We have a park near us?"

"Of course we do. It's why 90% of the people live in this neighborhood, because it's so perfect for families. Isn't that why you bought a house here?"

"Uh, no. I bought this house because my brother Peter said it had really good resale..." Dalton shook his head. "Peter," he said under his breath, the name almost a curse.

"What?"

"Nothing. You'd have to know my brother. He's one of those happy-endings-are-for-everyone kind of guys."

"And you're one of those—" she looked at the pages of the book again "—'he choked the life out of her' kind of guys?"

He chuckled. "Exactly."

"Maybe that's why you have that writer's block. You need some fresh air. People around you."

"It's not a block. It's..." His voice trailed off. The stress of the last few months, the frustration of sending pages to his editor that only ended up being torn apart and rejected, caught up with

Dalton. He let out a gust, and ran a hand through his hair. He'd been stuck in this house for three months, cut off from his friends, his family, everyone, except for Mrs. Winterberry, whose sole solution to Dalton's writer's block had been a tin of chocolate chip cookies. Good cookies, unfortunately not full of inspiration. "It's more of a…logjam. My writing has hit a wall of sorts."

Had he just admitted that? To a near stranger? He rarely talked about his work—and especially his lack of progress— to anyone.

Damned embarrassing, the whole thing. He, Dalton Scott, *New York Times* bestselling author, stuck and sinking deeper every day into a quagmire of bad writing—writing so awful, not even his agent—who was paid 15% to gush over everything Dalton wrote—could stomach.

"Because?"

He dropped into an armchair, the weight of his career, or current lack thereof, sitting heavy on his shoulders. "Because I seem to have a wonderful knack for writing 'unemotional, flat novels' to quote just one of the critics who reviewed my first book. And that was the *best* thing he said about it."

"Well, if there's one thing I have in abundance right now, it's emotions." Ellie let out a little laugh. "Too bad you can't peek into my head. I'd give you plenty to write about."

"Yeah, too bad." His editor had specifically mentioned that Dalton's female characters were the least well developed. He had to admit, he shied away from writing deeply about them. Give him a hard-boiled detective, a jaded cop, a sarcastic villain, and he'd write his fingers off. But a woman?

Dalton would rush past those pages, preferring any other kind of scene.

And he knew why. He wasn't much good with women. Hadn't he already proved that years ago with Julia? He'd lost her—

Lost everything. Because when it had come to crunch time, he'd let her go. He'd walked away. Maybe he hadn't really had a choice, or maybe he had.

Either way, he wouldn't go there. He had no desire to get close to a woman again. Not even to take a "peek inside her head," as Ellie had said.

He'd find another way to finish the book. A less involved way.

"You know what you need?" Ellie said, interrupting his thoughts. "The same thing I need."

The craziest thought popped into Dalton's head just then, as he looked into Ellie Miller's wide green eyes. His gaze dropped to her curvy figure, and a charge of desire ran through him. He might not want to peek inside her mind, or get involved, but it had been a long time since he'd been involved with a woman and every ounce of testosterone in his body was reminding him—very insistently—of that fact.

What did he need right now?

A kiss. Maybe a little more.

"Uh…what are you talking about?" he asked, pushing those thoughts away.

"A break." She smiled. "I think both of us could use some fresh air. You're about as pale as death warmed over."

"Thanks. Glad to know you find me so attractive. Maybe I should go around with my back cover photo pasted on my face."

She paused, and a flush crept into her cheeks. "Oh, I didn't say…I didn't mean…"

Ellie was flustered. Desire raged in Dalton's veins, rushing so fast, the feeling took him completely by surprise. He hadn't had a woman in his house in a long time. A long, long time. And here this one came along, and upset a totally perfect balance. "Of course you didn't."

Then she recovered, and that feisty gleam was back in her emerald eyes. "All I meant was, we should play a little hooky." She put out her hand. "Are you game, Dalton Scott?"

He hesitated only a second, then took her palm in his, wondering if he was doing the right thing. When he touched Ellie, a nearly electric pulse traveled up Dalton's arm. Something he could almost call attraction, if he'd been in the business of being attracted to a woman. A woman with a kid, no less.

And that told Dalton he was getting way more than he bargained for in this deal. Something he hadn't been prepared for—and a bonus he wasn't so sure he wanted.

Ellie Miller was apparently a pro at the picnic thing. Dalton stood by in amazement as she bustled around his kitchen, getting the baby tucked into a stroller, along with what seemed like a year's worth of supplies jammed into a diaper bag. She had raided his fridge for ingredients for a late lunch, and packed them into a cooler he unearthed from the garage.

At the last minute, despite her mantra about needing a break, Ellie had packed her calendar and her notepad, along with the cell phone that never stopped. Even as they were walking out the door and rounding the corner of her street, toward the park, she was arguing with someone about lighting their facial features or some such thing, leaving Dalton to push the kid.

Making him feel altogether way too much like the father in this little trio, and not at all what he had intended when he agreed to go along on this expedition. The pink striped stroller rolled along the sidewalk, the kid cooing happily, while neighbors sent them friendly smiles and waves. As if he, Ellie and the kid were just another family heading toward the park.

As soon as Ellie ended the call, Dalton transferred the handles to her grip. "You push this. It's your kid, after all."

"You're the babysitter." She tossed him a grin. Rays of sunshine bounced off her delicate features. Below them, the kid was singing an endless tune of ba-ba-ba. "I'm just along to make sure you don't cheat and turn around after five minutes."

"Look who's talking."

"What are you talking about?"

He gestured toward her cell phone. "You might as well have glued that phone to your hand. I thought we'd agreed to play hooky."

"We are, when we get to the park." She gestured the few hundred yards toward the entrance. "It's just up there."

He snorted. "I'm calling you on a technicality, Miss Miller."

"That's not a technicality, it's a reality. I still have a few details to sew up before the end of the day. If I don't work, I don't pay the rent. If I don't pay the rent, Sabrina and I are homeless—"

"I thought *I* was the fiction writer. You can

afford to take a half an hour off to go to the park, including the five minutes it takes to walk there and back. And you know it."

She opened her mouth to protest. Shut it again. Opened it, shut it. Gave him a glare, then finally turned the phone off and tucked it away, deep inside the diaper bag. "Thirty minutes. Any more, and the company I work for will send out a search party."

He laughed.

"I'm not kidding."

Sabrina punctuated the statement with a ba-ba-ba and a rattle shake, as if she had her own personal set of cymbals.

"Makes me glad I don't have a real job. I don't think I could take a boss breathing down my neck like that."

"I'd give about anything to work at home all day like you do. But in my industry, that's just not feasible." She sighed.

"Then why are you in that industry?"

She shrugged. "I sort of…fell into it. I met Cameron, and he needed an assistant, and he hired me. I stayed, and got promoted, and here I am. Working a million hours a week."

Cameron. The name perked Dalton's attention. Was Cameron the missing baby's father? Or someone else? He wanted to ask, but told himself it was none of his business. He was here for a couple days at most, to help her out, then get back to his private, non-social life. That was all.

As they entered the park, a cacophony of small children surrounded them. Kids everywhere—climbing on the bright playground equipment, swinging on the swings, running on the wide expanse of grass, dodging each other among the trees. Playing in the huge sandbox shaded by a red-and-white striped awning. Dotted around the area were mothers, chatting together and dispensing hugs and snacks as needed.

Dalton seemed to be the lone man. He couldn't have felt more out of place if he'd walked into a lingerie store on bra fitting day.

"Let's go over here," Ellie said, pointing toward a small bench under a wide oak tree. "It's in the shade."

They settled the stroller to the side, the baby now asleep, then Ellie sat. He plopped down beside her, unable to shake that feeling that the image they presented was surely Family on an Outing.

"You going to take her on the swings or anything?" he asked. Anything to get them off this bench and moving.

"She's too small for the ones they have here and they don't have a baby swing. Maybe I'll take her on the slide after lunch, if the bigger kids are done. Either way, Bri just likes being outside. So do I." Ellie tipped her face to meet the sky above. Dappled rays sneaking through the blanket of leaves kissed her skin like golden jewels. "Let me just enjoy this for a minute before we eat. And you can get a chance to relax, too."

"Uh, yeah, relax." Easier said than done when he realized how very aware of her he was.

She was beautiful. Almost…luminescent.

He chided himself. What was he doing? Pulling out a mental thesaurus? He really needed to get out more or something.

Dalton put one arm on the back of the bench, and shifted his position. Put his ankle across the opposite knee. Dropped the foot down again. Turned his hip, tried another seating arrangement for his backside. And found comfortable, and being beside a beautiful woman like Ellie, didn't go together. "I'm not really a park bench kind of guy."

Her eyes were closed now, her head leaned against the back of the bench, the expression on her face as serene as a lake on a summer day. "Then what kind of guy are you?" she asked, her voice lazy, quiet.

The kind who wanted to kiss her right now. Who wanted to absorb just a little of whatever it was that she had found, that peace. That sweetness.

He'd definitely been working too much. Been, as she'd said, cooped up way too long.

He leaned over, searching her face, seeing the absence of lines, of stress, wondering how the heck she had gone from sixty to zero in such a short period. He reached up a hand—inches from her ivory skin, so close, he could feel the slight heat emanating from her, catch the slight scent of raspberries in her perfume—but not quite close enough to touch her.

Her eyes opened and she jerked up, narrowing the distance between them. "What are you doing?"

"Uh…" What was he supposed to say? How would he explain this? "Nothing."

Then he sat back against the bench again, before he gave in to the crazy ideas in his brain, ideas that came from too much sunshine.

And not enough sense.

CHAPTER FOUR

FOR a second, Ellie had thought Dalton was going to kiss her, but at the very last second, he drew back. Two emotions rocketed through her.

Relief. And disappointment.

She didn't need a man in her life, a complication like that, but oh, the loneliness that wrapped around her every night in her bed, had seemed to quadruple at that moment. She had wanted him to kiss her very much.

But then he had sat back, and she'd decided she'd misread the move. It had been a long time since a man had made a move on her, so a little misreading was an easy thing for her to do.

There were times—times like this one—when being a widow hit her square in the gut. When she was reminded all over again of all she had lost and how much it hurt. When she was forced to deal with the loss of her husband, and how she was no longer one of two.

But just one.

Ellie blinked back a few tears, and told herself she would think about that later. Those words had become her mantra over the last few months. Later, later, later.

Yeah, like when Sabrina was eighteen.

They sat there for a moment, both of them pretending to watch the groups of children climbing up and down the jungle gyms. Beside them, Sabrina kept on sleeping. No timely distraction would be coming from the baby, not now. "Mrs. Winterberry tells me you come from a family of twelve," Ellie said, if only to break up the tension with a change of topic.

"Mrs. Winterberry talks too much."

"She said that's where you got all your…baby experience." Ellie arched a brow. "Such as it is."

"Are you saying you don't think I'm good with kids? Or in your case, one kid?"

"Well, you're not exactly Mr. Warm and Fuzzy."

"No one said you have to be warm and fuzzy to watch a kid. I don't remember it being in the babysitter manual."

"Since when have you ever read a babysitting manual?"

A flush filled his cheeks and Ellie realized she'd just exposed a vulnerable side of Dalton Scott. Well, well. She waited, watching him, letting silence press him into filling in the blanks. It took several long seconds, but finally he did.

"Hey, my sister left one lying around once. A guy can get desperate for reading material sometimes." He shot her a quick glance. "That's my story and I'm sticking to it."

She laughed. "And was the Evil Eye that silences small children an inherited trait, or a tip in the book, too?"

"That," Dalton said, wagging a finger at her, "was one I developed on my own. Call it…a survival tactic."

"Survival tactic? Surviving what?"

"What does it matter?"

"I'm just curious," she said.

He scowled. "Let's just drop it. I'm helping you out for a couple days, I'm not moving in and become dad, okay?"

A glacier had moved between them, and clearly, there'd be no moving it, no taking it down. Conversation over.

"Yeah, sure," she said.

He got to his feet and swung away from the bench, putting several steps of distance between them. Clearly, what they had been talking about had hit some kind of nerve. Odd.

She didn't need to care. Or get involved. Dalton's life was his own. She had her own to worry about. And that, right now, was enough. Still, the worry nagged at her, and she found her gaze straying to him, to the lone tall figure silhouetted against the bright summer sun.

What had happened to him? What had made him so… hardened?

There had to be more to it than the typical hermit writer. But what, Ellie didn't know. Either way, Dalton wasn't talking, and she wasn't asking.

She shrugged off the thoughts, reached under the stroller for a blanket, then pulled out the small cooler they had packed earlier. "I'd say it's time to eat, wouldn't you?"

He turned back, the perpetual scowl back on his face. "I'm not hungry right now."

"Well, I am. In fact, I'm starving. And you probably are, too, considering you missed lunch when I was there earlier." She propped a fist on her hip, determined to change the subject and perhaps tease him back to where they'd been before. "Now if you're done being grumpy, you can join Sabrina and me. We prefer *pleasant* dining companions." Then she turned on her heel, taking the stroller over to the shade of the oak tree a few feet away.

As soon as she stopped moving, the baby woke up, putting out her arms, clamoring to be held. Ellie smiled and reached for Sabrina. This was where her priorities lay. Not with a relationship. She couldn't juggle both, along with a job, and the bills, and the stress of all she had gone through. She'd concentrate on Bri, and work, and leave it at that. It would be enough for now.

It had to.

She held her daughter tight for a few minutes, then went to put her back into the stroller, to have her hands free for setting up the picnic. But as soon as Ellie did, Bri started crying. There'd be none of that, the baby declared with her lungs, not while her mother was there and had available arms.

Balancing Bri on one hip, Ellie bent down, got the blanket, and unfurled it, the plaid catching the slight breeze and waving the cloth into a rectangle. But as Ellie tried to settle it onto the ground, the wind worked against her, folding the corners onto themselves. The baby squirmed in her arms, wanting to be down on the ground—now—only complicating matters.

"Bri, I have to put you down, honey." She moved toward the stroller again, but Sabrina figured out what was coming, and clutched at her mother's shoulder. Nope. Not going there. No way, not now.

Ellie tried the one-armed blanket move again, and got no further than she had the first time. She let out a gust, and wished she could grow a third arm. How did other moms make these jobs look so easy?

"Here. Let me do that. You're going to dislocate a shoulder or something." Dalton took the end from her, and in one swift movement, had the blanket laid out, neat and smooth.

Ellie smiled her gratitude. "Are you joining us now?"

"It's either you or the hordes of small and dangerous humans over there." He thumbed toward the playground. "I'd rather take my chances with the stinky screamer." He gestured toward Sabrina.

"Bri's not a stinky screamer. She's a baby. All babies smell. And cry."

"I know babies. And yours smells the worst. Not to mention, cries the loudest. In fact, I've already scheduled a hearing test for next week."

She should have been offended, but his words had lost their bite, especially because a hint of a smile played around his lips when he said them. The scowl had left, and whatever storm had been brewing from before had passed. Perhaps Sabrina was growing on him. Or maybe Ellie had just gotten too tired to care. "So tell me, what's so dangerous about a bunch of preschoolers?"

"Let's just say a grown man shouldn't get anywhere near them and playground equipment. They're all just the right height to inflict permanent damage."

"Do you ever look at your glass as half-full?"

He cocked a grin at her. "Only when it's half-full of whiskey."

She chuckled. "You are incorrigible."

"And you sound like my mother."

"If I was your mother, I'd be making sure you had healthier food in your fridge." She pulled out the store-made potato salad, the bologna sandwiches they'd made earlier, along with a bag of chips and two cans of soda. Behind them, the high-pitched squeals of happy, playing children rose and fell. Birds fluttered from tree to tree and a soft breeze played with the leaves. The day couldn't have been more perfect if it had been painted and hung in the Louvre. "How can you eat this stuff day after day?"

"For your information, bologna is a meat. I think. Bread is from the bread group, and potato salad has some vegetables in it." Dalton peered into the plastic container. "They're just cut up so tiny you probably can't see them."

"Next you'll be trying to tell me the soda is a sports drink, filled with so many electrolytes and vitamins, they forgot to put them on the label."

"Hey, you never know what they put in that stuff. Read the can. Lots of mysterious ingredients in there." He grinned.

When Dalton Scott smiled, something zinged in Ellie's chest. Something that hadn't zinged in a really long time. Not since Cameron. The feeling was so foreign, so strange, she didn't know how to handle it. How to react.

It was almost as if she'd had a baby and then forgotten how to be a woman. How to date. How to flirt.

Was this flirting? Or was she completely misreading every signal Dalton Scott was sending?

Dalton was so different from Cameron, who'd been quieter, less unpredictable. And not a man filled with all these mysteries. Depths she couldn't seem to plumb. And wasn't so sure she wanted to.

Either way, what she was going to do—what was smart to do—right now, was eat. Not think about getting involved with another man again, when she'd barely had time to take a breath after losing her husband.

"Here's some, uh, forks," Ellie said, digging deeper into the cooler and pulling out a plastic zip-bag filled with paper plates, napkins, and utensils. Dalton hadn't had any idea where those were in his house, and it had taken some digging on Ellie's part to find what she considered picnic necessities. Clearly, the man wasn't a picnic regular. As for her, it had been so long since she'd been on one, she'd nearly forgotten the sweet joy of being outside.

Right now, though, with Dalton so close to her on the blanket, a little leaning one way or another would cause her to touch him. Heat emanated from his skin, and electricity hummed between them. Try as she might not to be aware, Ellie was. Very much aware. Of everything. The woodsy scent of his cologne. The deep blue of his eyes. The way his dark hair curled over the collar of his shirt, making her ache to run her fingers through those longish ends. To feel the strength of a man against her body, to be held again.

Specifically to be held by *him*. His lean, muscular frame.

She cleared her throat and reached inside the cooler. "Here's um, a plate, napkin—" she handed each thing to him "—paper cup… Do you need anything else?"

He put the towering stack onto the blanket. "Do I make you nervous?"

"No, of course not. Why would you say that?"

"Because you just called the paper cup a napkin. And the napkin a paper plate." That grin again, only this time it teased her.

"The baby distracted me." Yeah, blame it on the baby. Ellie shifted Sabrina to her lap. "Would you like some…some potato salad?"

The grin widened. "Sure. Let me get it. Seems you have your hands full."

That and her brain. The man had read her like a phone book. Ellie concentrated on smoothing her napkin across her lap, wishing she could make her thoughts as blank as the white paper.

Dalton dished up the food, giving each of them generous portions. Ellie dug in, thinking she wasn't that hungry—since Sabrina had been born, she'd barely had time to sleep, never mind eat—but as soon as the food hit her palate, her hunger awakened, and she had cleaned her plate in record time, even working one-handed, and having to avoid a curious baby with waving fists.

"Your mother would be proud," Dalton said, giving her another of his teasing glances. "Not a bite left."

Heat filled her cheeks. Geez, she'd eaten even faster than Dalton had. "Half the time, I'm too busy to eat or too tired to cook anything. And when I do get a chance to eat, it's very rarely junk food."

"Well then, welcome to my world. It's all junk food, all the time."

"That explains it," she said quietly, nuzzling Sabrina's fuzz of hair.

"Explains what?"

"Why your happiness quotient is near zero. You're probably deficient in every major vitamin and mineral."

He pressed a hand to his chest, mocking a swoon. "Oh, Ellie. I didn't know you cared."

"I just don't want you having a heart attack in the middle of a diaper change."

He grinned.

She hadn't started to care about him, not even after he'd opened that little mysterious window this afternoon, she told herself. He was still, for all intents and purposes, a stranger. Granted, a stranger who had awakened a growing attraction inside her, but a man she barely knew all the same.

Either way, Dalton represented a complication and Ellie definitely didn't need one of those.

Sabrina started to squirm and fuss, so Ellie put her down on the blanket. Bri popped her head up, studying Dalton with wide eyes and a drooly, happy mouth. She had her little fists propped beneath her chest, as if she were to crawl away at any second. "Ba-ba-ba."

"Don't be thinking I'm going to share," Dalton said, glancing down at her and wagging his sandwich in the baby's direction.

She gasped. "You wouldn't honestly feed her a sandwich, would you?"

"Even I know babies don't eat sandwiches." He rolled his eyes. "Until they're at least a year old, right, kid?"

Ellie gasped.

"Kidding, kidding."

"Not so funny."

"You need to lighten up a bit, Ellie. Get some stress off."

"Easy for you to say. You work at home."

"Yeah, well, my job is not as unstressful as it looks." He took another bite of sandwich, effectively ending the subject. Dalton rested one arm across his knee and watched the kids playing for a moment. "So what made you go into this TV thing? You don't seem to like it much. I mean, I know you got promoted and all that. But what made you choose that field?"

"Why are you so interested? Last I checked you were pretty busy putting up those personal No Trespassing signs." Earlier today, she'd been glad for those. Staying impersonal kept the two of them from getting any closer—the best choice for her for now, and for the foreseeable future.

Even if he'd piqued her curiosity a minute ago. But she wasn't going to go there. Wasn't going to ask Dalton questions she couldn't answer for herself.

He quirked a half grin at her. "Sorry. Occupational hazard. Always trying to figure out what makes people tick."

She dug at her potato salad, picking at the remains on the plate, but finding nothing much to eat. "As clichéd as it sounds, I thought I could make a difference. That something I would produce would actually be important. I mean, it's what I went to college for, when I got a journalism degree. I didn't really envision going into television, but once I got there, I thought maybe I could produce a show that would…"

"Change the world?"

She shrugged. "Yeah. How naïve is that?" It had been a crazy dream. One of those college idealistic ones that everyone who graduates seems to have—and she'd been foolish enough to hold on to for way too long.

"Not so naïve." He shrugged. "I know the feeling."

"You mean you wanted to do the same with your books?"

He got to his feet, crumpling his paper plate into a ball. "Thanks for bringing the food. Sometimes when I'm deep into the writing, I forget to eat, so that was a good idea." He crossed to one of the trash cans and tossed the ball into the wooden rimmed barrel.

Another avoidance of a topic. Ellie told herself she didn't care. She wasn't here to get to know him. She wasn't, in fact, here for some extended vacation, either. She'd been at the park long enough, soaking up the sun, and allowing Sabrina to enjoy some time with her mother.

Before she got back to work.

While Bri rolled around on the blanket, and wriggled from one side to the other, cooing and gurgling while she moved, Ellie packed up the food. She replaced everything in the cooler, then loaded it into the stroller. Finally, she picked up Sabrina and strapped her into the seat, handing the baby a rattle as she did. The baby kicked happily, a wide grin on her face. "Enjoyed that, didn't you?"

Sabrina cooed.

"Maybe I finally found the key to you and I getting along, huh? If that's the case, we'll have to come back," Ellie said. Soon, she vowed. Soon.

Somehow, she'd find the time to add more trips to the park. To add more sunshine. More picnics. She'd find a way to make this balance even out more in Sabrina's favor. She had to.

This afternoon's temporary arrangement with Dalton, for all the complications it brought with Dalton himself, had had that added bonus of giving Ellie the gift of time with her daughter. She'd have to remember to thank him. When he was far away from her—so she wasn't tempted to kiss him like she had been just a little while ago.

Before she could reach for the blanket, Dalton was there, the folded cloth in his hands. He gave it to her, his larger palm brushing against hers as he did. A surge ran through her veins, telling herself distance was, indeed, the best choice all around.

Except she'd had the brilliant idea of working inside his house, and distance wasn't exactly easy to come by when she was sharing twenty-eight hundred square feet of space with the man.

"Leaving already?" he asked.

"I have to get back to your house and get some more work done." She sighed. "As it is they're probably sending out a search party, since my cell phone has been off for so long."

"Well, you did keep up your end of the bargain," Dalton said. "Let me go back to watching the kid for a while, and you can come back out of hiding." He put his hands on the stroller and started pushing. Bri kept on kicking and cooing, happy to be moving and walking.

"Thank you."

He shrugged. "Just doing my job."

Every once in awhile, he did something like that and totally surprised her. She didn't get it. Either he hated being a babysitter or not. Disliked being around kids or he didn't. And what caused him to sometimes step in, without being asked, and just take over like that?

Whatever it was, she shouldn't question Dalton's motives, Ellie decided, as she powered up her cell phone.

Because there were eight messages waiting for her. Telling her she may have gotten a slight respite, but she was going to pay for those moments. And therefore find herself even further behind—and further away from Sabrina and her ultimate goal than ever before.

What on earth possessed him to do these things?

Five minutes ago, he was hands-off, belly full, ready to head home, and avoid Ellie and this whole thing the rest of the day. Tell Ellie she could use his house as a home office, as long as she left him alone.

But then she'd gone and become *relatable* for Pete's sake, and something in his heart had cracked open.

For a man who didn't think his heart was capable of cracking open—at least not ever again—that was a new feeling. And not one he was sure he welcomed.

So here he found himself doing, of all things, pushing a baby stroller down the street. If his mother could see him now, she'd probably break out the video camera and start filling the family photo album to mark the occasion.

The kid kept looking up at him through the clear square peek-hole of the stroller's sunshade, as if she wanted to keep making sure it was really Dalton behind the wheel. Her blue eyes looked like little saucers, accented by rosy apple cheeks.

"What are you looking at?" he said, but his voice had lost its gruff edge.

Must have been all that potato salad.

Ellie had fallen a few steps behind, working her cell phone, her voice as busy as her fingers. That left him and the kid alone. Geez. All he needed now was a Golden Retriever and this would be the perfect family set-up.

He cast a glance over his shoulder at Ellie and caught her watching the kid while she talked. Every time she looked at her baby, her face softened. Not like melting ice cream, Dalton thought, searching for the right description, but like—

Like silk settling over diamonds. Every hard surface became smooth, everything about her—everything which was already beautiful—became even more beautiful.

His pulse sputtered, his breath caught.

He had the sudden urge to stop right there, right in the center of Elm Street, and start writing, to try to capture every word of the way she looked. The way her heart had been written across her features.

But of course he couldn't do that. For one, he had nothing with him to write with. And for another, Ellie—and all the neighbors who were out weeding their gardens or tending their lawns—would undoubtedly think the reclusive author was even more crazy than they'd already rumored him to be.

So he spun back around and started pushing the stroller a little faster. Get back to his house, and get back to his office. Then he could try to capture those words—in private. Where he liked to be. All this being around people stuff was overrated.

"Out for a power walk today, or what?" Ellie asked, catching up to him with a light jog.

"Just thought it would be easier for you to work if we were back at my house."

"Actually…" Ellie gave him a hopeful smile. "It turns out my boss decided on a drinks meeting tonight with the head brass about next week's show, and he's made it mandatory that I attend. Would you mind terribly watching Sabrina for a little while longer? I'll pay you for the overtime."

On his own? With the kid again? Every time he seemed to come close of ridding himself of this kid, he got suckered into keeping her.

But this time he was stronger. And Ellie wasn't crying. He was putting his foot down, and saying no. "No can do. I don't need the money. What I need is to work on my book."

Ellie thought a second. "What if I sweeten the pot?"

They'd arrived at the front of his house. Dalton opened the door and stepped inside, helping her wrangle the stroller over the threshold, before speaking again. He had to take a second to absorb those words, because a whole lot of ideas about how exactly she could sweeten the pot were racing through his mind—and they were probably not at all what Ellie had in mind. It had to be all that sunshine, coupled with that insane moment back on the bench when he'd almost kissed her. "And how do you propose to do that?"

"I stop for groceries on the way back and make you a proper dinner. I saw—and dined on—the contents of your refrigerator. That's no way for a human to live. So I was thinking—" she clasped her hands together "—how does homemade spaghetti and meatballs sound?"

Ellie here. In his kitchen, making him dinner. How did that sound?

Like having heaven walk in his front door.

"Depends," he said. "What do you call homemade?"

"Made from scratch. Everything."

His mouth began to water. When was the last time he'd had a homemade meal? Since he'd left home at nineteen…he could probably count on one hand the number of homemade meals he'd had that hadn't come at his mother's dining table during a holiday.

"Is there a dessert involved in this offer?"

"Are you accepting?"

His stomach made the response before his

better sense could. "As long as you don't believe in parmesan cheese that comes out of a can, I'm all yours."

CHAPTER FIVE

THE scents of oregano and basil filled the house, coupled with the sharp notes of Parmesan cheese. Ellie stood in Dalton's gourmet kitchen—a room that didn't get much use, if the pristine condition of his granite countertops and gas cooktop was any indication—and tended to a pan of frying meatballs while the tomato sauce simmered in a separate pot.

At the table, Sabrina sat in a portable high chair Ellie had brought over, and banged on the table. What had been happy slaps a moment ago was soon accompanied by a series of high-pitched demanding shrieks. "I think she wants some meatballs," Dalton said.

"She's a little young for those. I've got strained peas and mashed bananas on Bri's menu tonight. Can you feed her so I can finish this?"

He stared at Ellie. "Me?"

"It's easy. Well, easy-ish." Ellie gave him a

grin. She figured she'd leave off the warnings about spitting peas and regurgitated bananas or Dalton would never feed Bri. "Just put on her bib and use the tiny spoon to feed her. I'd alternate peas and bananas."

He fitted the bib around Sabrina's neck. "Why alternate?"

"She hates peas. The bananas are a bribe."

He chuckled. "So that's how my mother got me to eat my vegetables."

"That's how all mothers do it, I suspect. It's a tip I learned from Mrs. Winterberry." Ellie took a step back from the stove and then flipped a few meatballs to brown their other sides. "I was having a heck of a time getting Sabrina to eat anything other than cereal. Thank goodness Mrs. Winterberry was there to help me through those rough spots. Some days, I feel…" She blew a lock of hair off her face. "Well, it's just hard to be alone."

A soft pop sounded in the room—the top on the baby jar releasing. Dalton held Ellie's gaze for a long moment. "Where is he?"

"Who?"

"Bri's father."

She pushed at a meatball, watching the browned meat turn and spin on the pan. "He died when I was pregnant."

Died.

The word hit Dalton hard. He'd expected Ellie to say a hundred different things. That the man had run off, left her alone. Or that he was out of the picture for some other selfish reason. But to hear that final tone in Ellie's voice, the grief that lingered in the heavy syllable, made him want to leap out of the chair and—

Well, hold her. Comfort her.

But he wasn't the holding or comforting type. So he stayed where he was, even as that urge grew in his chest.

He opened his mouth to say something when Sabrina slapped the table, letting out an emphatic demand for the food in Dalton's hands. He dipped the rubber-tipped spoon into the jar and held the green soupy mess toward the baby. She opened her mouth eagerly, then made a face when she tasted the peas.

Ellie laughed. "Better get the bananas ready or she'll be spitting back the second bite."

He did as Ellie suggested, sending a spoonful of bananas in next. Bri bounced happily in response. Before she could see the green, he snuck in some peas, then followed her swallow with some bananas. In between bites, he said, "I'm…I'm sorry, Ellie."

"You're doing fine with her."

"I meant about Sabrina's father."

"Oh. Thank you. I never thought my story, or

Bri's, would end this way." She turned back to the stove, stirring the meatballs for a long time. Again, sympathy rocked him. She'd probably hardly had a second since she'd had this kid—a kid who took tons of time in Dalton's opinion—to deal with losing the kid's father.

"Who says it ended?"

She pivoted toward him. "What do you mean?"

"Just because he died doesn't mean your story is over." He grinned. "Take it from the fiction writer. You can always create a new chapter." He gave the baby some more peas, using the spoon to wipe off what didn't make it into her mouth.

"Dalton, you don't understand. When Cameron died, it was…devastating. My whole life turned upside down. Every plan I had for my life, for my baby's life, it all changed. Now I'm juggling everything, all alone, and most days I feel like I'm doing a terrible job of it. He left me with no life insurance, no rudder, left me to just—" she threw up her hands "—be everything by myself. Both parents, breadwinner, decision maker. I don't have *time* to write a new chapter, never mind find someone to star in it with me."

"You're not doing so bad. Your kid's all right." He gave the baby another spoonful of peas.

Ellie shrugged, then smiled a little. "Are you saying she's growing on you?"

Just then Sabrina realized he'd broken his promise and fed her two spoonfuls of peas in a row. She spat the second spoonful back, straight into Dalton's face. He scowled and swiped them off, spitting out the bland green vegetable. "Something like that."

Ellie laughed. And laughed. And laughed. Dalton found himself joining in, even though the experience hadn't been funny at the time. The feeling of laughter was oddly light, and, well, nice. He shook his head, and marveled at these two females who had come into his house and turned it upside down in ways he hadn't wanted or expected. But was finding he didn't mind as much as he'd thought.

A few minutes later, the baby was fed, dinner was done, and Dalton was pea-free. The mood had shifted away from their conversation about the past, and into one far more jovial, as if Sabrina's pea spitting had changed everything. Ellie filled a plate with steaming spaghetti noodles, topping them with a generous dollop of sauce and several meatballs, then turned to Dalton. "Fresh Parmesan cheese?"

"You're speaking my language, honey." He gave his stomach a pat.

She laughed. "I guess I don't even need to ask about garlic bread."

"Don't you know you're supposed to feed writers? It's part of supporting the arts."

She grinned, and added an extra slice of bread to his plate, then handed him his dinner. Beside the table, Sabrina played happily in the portable playpen Ellie had also brought over from her house. That gave Ellie time to grab a plate and sit down across from Dalton at the round glass table.

As soon as she did, the strangeness of the situation slammed into her. She hadn't had a meal with a man in over a year. Not since Cameron. Speaking about him earlier made the loss slam into her, as if a tidal wave had been sitting behind a wall of rocks, waiting for a moment like this.

Ellie had told herself all these months that there would be time. Time to deal with the hole in her heart, the hole in her life. But ever since Cameron had died, there'd been too many things in the way to find that time. Her pregnancy, work, the bills, and now Sabrina. Being here with Dalton and talking about Cameron forced her to deal with the loss. With her grief. With the fact that she hadn't thought she'd be doing this—sitting at a table, like a family, ever again.

But they weren't a family, were they? This was a working relationship. Albeit, a highly unconventional one. Still, she couldn't help but notice how *easy* it all felt, especially when they'd laughed together. How she could forget for a moment why she was really here.

And slip into the fantasy that she had come home after a long day at work, and so had Dalton, to form this perfect little family of three. Just like she had always dreamed of having for Sabrina. Just like she had set out to have.

"You're not eating," Dalton said.

"Sorry. I, ah, got distracted." She toyed with her fork. "Maybe this is a good time for us to lay down some ground rules."

"Ground rules?" He quirked a brow. "Isn't this my house? Therefore, my rules?"

"If we're going to be working together, even for a few hours, I have a few of my own."

He sat back against his chair. "Let me guess. You're one of those 'use a coaster every time you have a drink,' and 'no shoes in the house' kind of women. You have a heart attack if I leave crumbs on the countertop. Am I right?"

She laughed. "No. You're wrong."

He leaned closer. "Then what kind are you?"

She told herself she didn't mind him narrowing the gap between them. Her heartbeat didn't accelerate one bit. It was hormones. Nothing more.

Because she hadn't had a man in her life in over a year. And even if Dalton had said she could write a new chapter, she wasn't about to start now. Regardless of how blue his eyes were, or how the storms brewing in them had her questioning for the first time if there was, indeed, something missing in her life.

"I'm the kind who doesn't need any more complications than I already have," Ellie said.

"That," Dalton said, closing the gap, then widening it again, bringing a draft into the space between them, "is exactly the kind of woman I'm looking for."

"Good," she said, her mind still on Dalton, despite all she'd said, still thinking about how much this felt, not quite like a date, but like…

Normal. Like they were together, and they had done this a hundred times before. And how much a part of her was really enjoying that feeling. "I'm glad we have that settled."

Neither of them said anything for a little while, the silence punctuated by Sabrina's happy squeals and occasional squeak of a toy.

"I've never had a woman cook for me before. Except for my mother." Dalton twirled some spaghetti onto his fork. "Either I pick the wrong women to date or I've never won any of them over with my stellar personality."

"Could be the women," Ellie said. She grinned. "Or not."

"I'm simply not one of those touchy-feely types. And not one to get close to others."

"Why?"

"I'm a guy. Isn't that reason enough?"

"Even men open their hearts." She picked up a piece of garlic bread and dipped it into her sauce before taking a small bite. Even if they were treading on personal ground, Ellie figured it was worth the trade for having an actual adult to converse with. "If they want to have a relationship, or at least one that progresses beyond dinner."

He ate the spaghetti, chewed and swallowed. "Maybe I don't want one."

"You're happy being alone? Forever?"

"Maybe. For the foreseeable future, at least."

"Why?" Talk about two peas in a pod. Hadn't she just thought the exact same thing today?

Then why did a flicker of disappointment run through her? Why had she hoped Dalton would say the opposite?

Geez. She needed to get her hormones under control or something.

He gave her his trademark scowl. "You're like a three-year-old with that perpetual why thing."

"It's a valid question."

He wagged a piece of garlic bread in her direction. "One I could ask you just as easily. How long ago did your husband pass away?"

"A little over fifteen months." Gosh, had it really been that long? In some ways, it felt even longer. Especially when she was alone in the house, Sabrina gone to bed, and she realized how empty her life felt.

The small respite she'd had today—that half hour in the park—had done two things.

It had made her ache even more for what she couldn't have.

And made her wonder, in a small way, if it was possible to balance a life with the craziness that already comprised her world.

"Then what are you waiting for?" he asked. "Your kid to start college before you start dating?"

"I told you, I barely have time to do my laundry, never mind date." Ellie rose and walked away from the table, crossing to the sink, and covered for her emotions by starting the dishes.

She half expected Dalton to follow. To press her for more answers. But he didn't, and the silence seemed to question her even more. Why was she waiting? Why *was* she putting her life—and for that matter, Sabrina's—on hold even longer?

All she'd ever wanted for her little girl was the storybook ideal. A little house with a white picket fence. Maybe a dog. And most of all, a traditional family, a husband to come home to, a partner to help in raising their child.

But the husband had died before their child could be born, and the home had become a burden Ellie could barely hold on to. And as for her child?

Sabrina was getting less and less of her mother's attention every day, and with each sunrise, that storybook picture seemed more and more distant. Being with Dalton, she'd had a glimpse, a whisper of all she'd lost, but even more, a peek into the future, as if God had peeled back the curtain and said, "Here, Ellie, here is what you can have, if you only make the room."

The problem?

She had no idea how to make that space in her life, or most importantly, in her heart again.

Ellie gripped the edge of the sink, trying to will the tears away, to force them back. But they refused to go this time, like a watershed that had cracked.

Fat droplets plopped into the water, splashing onto the bubbles, popping them. Ellie swiped at her cheeks with the back of her hand. She was happy with her life, just the way it was. The rest would come in good time.

It would.

"You all right?"

Dalton behind her. His voice gruff.

"Sure. Just, ah, getting to these dishes before they…" There was no good reason to wash dishes right now. Not that she could think of.

"Dishes can wait. That's my theory. Especially when there's garlic bread to be eaten."

"You have it. I can have some later."

He put his hands on her shoulders and turned her away from the sink. She tried not to think about how steady, how dependable his grip on her felt but it was impossible. Tried not to look up into his blue eyes, but she couldn't resist. Tried not to feel cared for, cocooned, at that moment, as if she finally wasn't alone and could share all these fears and burdens, if only—

If only she dared.

"Eat your dinner," Dalton said. Then paused when he looked at her. "Why are you crying?"

"Nothing."

"I may not be Mr. Sensitive, but even I know people don't cry over nothing."

She slipped out of his grasp and went to Sabrina, lifting her out of the playpen. Better to focus on her daughter than on adding more to an already overloaded personal plate. "If you don't mind cleaning up the mess, I think I'll take Bri home now. I have a million things to do tonight."

"You're not avoiding the question, are you?"

She paused in the doorway, turning back toward him. "No more than you're avoiding mine." Then Ellie left.

Better not to answer than to confront what she couldn't—and didn't want to—answer. Especially not for herself.

* * *

"Dalton, I have good news and bad news."

Dalton leaned back in his black leather office chair, his feet up on his mahogany desk, and let out a sigh. "Let me guess, Reuben. The action's great. The emotion sucks."

At a paper-crowded desk in New York that Dalton had visited more than once over the course of his career, Reuben Banks chuckled. Dalton could picture him now—Reuben in a loud print Hawaiian shirt, his goatee perfectly groomed, short dark hair spiked and gelled into place. Reuben was unique, but intelligent—and damned good at his job. "You read my mind."

"You've said it often enough. I could write your cue cards for you." Dalton could also write the reviews that would undoubtedly be coming after this book's release. They'd be exactly like the last few. Acerbic, critical, and filled with single stars.

And they would not make his publisher happy. Or make his sales go up. Dalton let out a sigh.

"I probably don't need to tell you how important this book is. And how late it is, too. Production is breathing down my neck, Dalton. If you miss this deadline…"

Dalton could fill in those blanks, too. He'd be forcing his editor's hand—pretty much killing his own career. "Give me—" He wanted to say a week, but even he knew that was too ambitious, given how much work was left to do on the manuscript. "Two weeks."

Silence. "Two weeks it is. But this thing better be Michelangelo on paper when it arrives on my desk." Reuben hung up, leaving the pressure sizzling on the phone line.

Dalton pulled up the pages he'd sent Reuben by e-mail the other day and started reading them over. With the distance of a few days, he could see what his editor saw. The pages featuring the hero and heroine—and their love story—fell completely flat.

Dalton deleted it all. Tomorrow, he'd start fresh.

But the problem was, with what? Where would he find something to model his story on? And secondly, how would he capture those feelings on paper?

Then his doorbell rang, and when he crossed to the front door and opened it to let in Ellie Miller, he realized he'd been overlooking the perfect way to solve his problem.

"You want me to do what?"

"Help me write."

"But I'm no writer." She juggled the baby to the opposite hip, her lips going to the kid's head in an automatic gesture of nuzzling. A softening came over Ellie's features, her eyes half-closing for one second. Dalton watched her inhale, catching the kid's scent, before she drew back. He swore his heart skipped a beat.

If he'd been the kind of guy whose heart did that when he got around kids and women. Which he wasn't. Because he'd worked hard at steeling himself against that kind of thing. Call it self-preservation. Call it sealing off the artery before it could ever bleed again. He already knew that pain and had no desire to experience it again.

"Why would you want my help?" Ellie asked.

"You, ah, know about the one thing I'm not so good at."

"The only thing I know much about is TV shows." She glanced down at Sabrina. "And babies. And in that arena, I'm still pretty new." She smiled at her baby, and brushed a kiss across her cheek. The kid, content and fed, dozed against Ellie's shoulder.

"What you are good at is, well…" He paused, toed at the carpet, then forced the word out. "Love."

Ellie coughed. "Did you just say love?"

"It's something I…well, I kind of failed. And I can't seem to get those emotions—or heck, any emotions—on the page to save my life."

"And you think I can write about an emotion like love? Because why?"

"Because…" And now he stepped forward, as if

he could plumb the mysteries of that feeling right out of her eyes, and the way she held her child, and transpose them now onto the blank pages in his computer. "Because I see it every time you look at your kid. In the way you kiss her, hold her."

A quiet smile stole across Ellie's face. "Well, Sabrina does her part. Even when she's grumpy, she makes it pretty easy to love her."

"There. That right there," he said, narrowing the gap even further. "If I could get you to describe what you're feeling, then maybe I could work that into my work. And that would make my editor, and eventually, my readers, happy."

She shook her head. "I still don't get it. Do you have a baby in your story?"

He laughed. "Not at all. No kids ever appear in my books."

"Why not?"

"I just don't work well with them. On paper or off." Then he realized how that sounded, considering he'd taken on the job of temporary babysitter. "Except with your kid, of course."

"Of course." Her sarcastic grin told him how much she believed that addition. "Anyway, it's a nice idea, but I still don't see how I can help you. And, I have to get to work. Which means it's your turn to take Sabrina."

"What if—" he paused a second, formulating

the idea in his head "—you called in sick for a couple days, and worked for me instead?"

"Call in sick. Work for you." She repeated the words, flatly, in disbelief. "How could I afford that?"

"I'll pay you."

She let out a chuff of disbelief. "You can't afford to do that. And what exactly is it that you are paying me to do?"

"To help me with my book, like I said earlier." He sank into his chair and ran a hand through his hair. "Listen, I've got two weeks to finish this book. To make it into something amazing. Something that will sell. My last few books have…well, let's just say they've—"

"Tanked." She gave him an apologetic smile. "I know how to use Google."

She'd researched him. Well, well. Maybe Ellie was more attracted to him than Dalton had thought—or maybe he was just reading more into a simple computer search than he should. "Tanked is probably a compliment, but yeah."

"And if I don't help you?"

"My new book does just as badly as all the others, and I don't go back to contract, which means I'll eventually have to get a real job. And you know how well I get along with others, particularly grown-ups." She smiled, which he took as a sign he was wearing her down. "You're only as good as your last sale. And I haven't sold well in a long, long time. It's like—"

When he didn't continue, Ellie moved forward, shifting the baby's weight as she did. Sabrina tugged at Ellie's hair, winding her chubby fist in and out of the brunette locks. "Like what?"

He shook his head. "Nothing. I just need help. That's all."

She turned away and started to circle his office, patting the kid's back as she did. "If I call in sick, my boss will completely freak out. We're in the middle of producing next week's show and—"

"Can he live without you?"

She laughed. "He doesn't think so."

Dalton thought for a minute. "How much more work do you have to do to get this show ready to go?"

"On my end? Actually, *I'm* ready. I've got all my guests lined up. The rest is all fine-tuning. Making sure they have their bottles of Perrier and bowls of just green M&M's, those kinds of things."

"Then he *can* live without you."

"Maybe he could," she conceded.

"Right now, I can't. So that decides it." Though the words had come out as a joke—and had been intended as one—Dalton had closed the gap between himself and Ellie, and suddenly, it seemed as if what he meant had become ten times more serious. As if he'd stopped talking about his career and veered into other, deeper territory. Relationship grounds.

Which he definitely hadn't. He was talking books. Nothing more.

"I suppose I could take a few days off," Ellie said, dubiously.

"I'll take what I can get." He grinned. "And, if you promise to throw in another one of those homemade dinners, I'll call it even."

Ellie thrust out her hand. Dalton took it, noting the delicate bones, the way her skin mirrored silk against his rougher palm. "You have a deal, Mr. Scott."

When her deep green eyes met his, with their unplumbed depths, something turned over in his chest. And Dalton had to wonder just what kind of deal he'd just made.

CHAPTER SIX

"So," Mrs. Winterberry asked as way of saying hello, "how are things going with you and our handsome neighbor?"

A loaded question, if Ellie had ever heard one. No matter how she answered, the response required qualifying. So she stuck to one word. "Fine."

"Come now, you must have more to say than that. Dalton Scott is a man who requires more than a single 'fine.'" Mrs. Winterberry, Ellie could swear, giggled.

"I've been very busy working," Ellie said.

"My dear, you really need to take a break. Take time to smell the roses."

"I do. I mean, I did. I went on a picnic yesterday." As soon as the words left her mouth, Ellie cringed.

"With Dalton? Oh, my. That's wonderful!"

"Mrs. Winterberry, tell me the truth. Did you leave Sabrina with Dalton because you were hoping he and I would…well, date or something?

Because really, I simply don't have time for anything like that."

"Oh, no, not at all. I was in a pinch. And Dalton's the only neighbor home during the day. But if something does spring up between the two of you…" Mrs. Winterberry's voice trailed off on a hopeful note. "You really do need a man in your life."

"Nothing's going to happen. The man is…impossible."

"That's because he's had his heart broken. Mind you, I don't know all the details, just something his brother alluded to once when I ran into him outside Dalton's house. There was a woman, and it ended badly. I get the feeling there was something more involved than just a simple love affair gone awry, but whatever it is, I know Dalton has terrible regrets because he doesn't want to talk about it. Just try to be understanding, Ellie, and most of all, be patient."

Ellie was not about to get into a discussion of Dalton, or the potential of a relationship with him. She'd been up half the night, tossing and turning, thinking about Dalton—which, considering Sabrina had slept through the night, probably worn-out by all the fresh air after the trip to the park—had been a foolish waste of a good night's sleep. After all those hours, her conclusion had been the same as before she went to bed.

Getting any further involved with him wouldn't work.

Except, she was heading back to his house today. To spend the entire day with him. Working side-by-side. Avoiding the simmering attraction between them, and pretending it didn't exist, well…

That would be about as easy as not breathing all day.

"How's your sister doing?" Ellie asked, to head off any further questions from Mrs. Winterberry.

"She's doing much better, thank you. She had to have a stent put in yesterday, but she came out of the surgery with flying colors, and she should be out of the hospital here in New Hampshire in a few days. If you need me, I'll come home to Boston until she's released, but after that, she really needs someone to take care of her until she's completely back on her feet. She's seventy-five, you know. Not near as spry as me. I'm the younger of the two of us." Mrs. Winterberry laughed.

If Ellie had been hoping for a fast resolution, there clearly wouldn't be one. She needed another sitter. She couldn't ask Mrs. Winterberry to put Sabrina ahead of her sister. That wouldn't be fair. "No, you stay there. I've got this under control. Dalton and I worked out an arrangement."

They'd done no such thing, but she wasn't about to tell Mrs. Winterberry that. Instead, she'd simply find someone else, and pray she could be lucky and get another inexpensive interim baby-sitter. She'd call the local college. They often had a list of daytime sitters. No need to worry Mrs. Winterberry.

"I knew you would," Mrs. Winterberry said. "That man is a saint, I tell you. He's helped me out dozens of times, with never a complaint."

"Are we talking about the same man?"

Mrs. Winterberry laughed. "Why, dear, Dalton Scott is the nicest man I've ever met. You'll see. Just give him a chance. You might be surprised at how wonderful you find him to be. And my dear, you need to move on, it's time."

Ellie didn't contradict Mrs. Winterberry, because doing so would be disrespectful to a woman who had been nothing but generous and incredible to her and Sabrina. But if there was one thing Ellie knew to be true, it was that giving Dalton Scott a chance—especially with her heart—would be the biggest mistake of her life.

"Is there something I should know about you?" Peter held up the pacifier and grinned at Dalton.

Dalton ripped the plastic thing away from his brother and tossed it onto the coffee table. "No."

"Then where did that come from? I gotta say, it's the last thing I ever expected to see in your house. Even if this is the perfect house for a family, might I remind you." Peter dropped his tall thin frame into one of the leather armchairs, draping his arms over the sides.

"I had company yesterday. She brought her kid."

Peter arched a brow. Waited for Dalton to continue.

"That's all. There's no more to tell."

"There's always more to tell, little brother," Peter said. "Now, do I have to bring over the lie detectors, or are you going to tell me?"

The lie detectors, AKA, their sisters, who could ferret the truth out of a mute. They had followed their brothers everywhere when Dalton had lived at home, then run home to their mother and tattled on anything bad the boys had done. Thereby scoring brownie points, and sometimes even real brownies, for getting the boys nabbed for things like playing in the creek when they should have been doing yard work.

He loved his sisters—but he owed them some payback. Which was why he sent their kids drum sets for Christmas.

Dalton popped open two cans of soda, handed Peter one, then took a seat on the sofa and propped his feet up on the coffee table. "The woman is named Ellie Miller. She lives across the street. She needed a temporary babysitter and being that I'm the only one around during the day, I got elected."

"But you don't do babysitting. You avoid kids like the black plague."

"It's only for a couple days." Dalton took a sip of soda. "No big deal."

"Uh-huh. You're getting involved. Coming out of the hermit cave. I'm proud of you." Peter leaned forward, scooped up the pacifier, and juggled it in his palm. "And with a woman who has a kid? I'd say this is a big, big deal."

Dalton shrugged.

"Is she pretty?"

Dalton scowled. "What does that have to do with anything?"

Peter chuckled. "She must be gorgeous. You're trying so hard to pretend you don't care. I think the man doth protest too much."

"And I think you're sticking your nose in way too much."

That only made Peter laugh some more. "So, are you going to take a chance this time, little brother?"

"What's that supposed to mean?"

"You know what I mean. Just because one relationship went down the sewer pipe of life doesn't mean you have to close yourself off to everyone else. You deserve a second chance, you know."

Dalton dropped his feet to the floor. "You don't

know what you're talking about. And I'm not looking for a relationship, either."

Peter glanced out the window, and let out a low whistle. "Wow. Is that the neighbor you're *not* getting involved with? The same one who doesn't have your attention at all?"

Dalton followed Peter's gaze. Ellie was coming across the street, Sabrina perched on her hip. Ellie had put on a deep brown floral print skirt today, one that flared out around her knees, exposing a great set of legs. Kitten heels accentuated her calves, while a short-sleeved off-white sweater outlined the rest of her curves.

Damn. Dalton wasn't going to get a single thing done today, that was for sure. Why couldn't the woman have worn sweats and a T-shirt like other people who worked at home? Or jeans and a T-shirt, like he had chosen?

Then another thought occurred to him. Had she chosen the skirt and sweater for him? Because she—

Liked him?

The thought should have bothered him. Should have had him upset, because he had just gotten through telling Peter no way, no how, was he getting involved with a woman again. But it didn't. Instead, the thought that Ellie might have had him in mind when she went through her closet today, that she had considered his reaction when she'd opted for the skirt, sent a thrill racing through his veins.

"Yeah, you're not interested one bit," Peter whispered in his ear. Then he laughed, and dropped the pacifier into Dalton's palm.

Ellie had taken the coward's way out. Twice.

She'd called in sick by leaving a message with Connie, who hadn't believed for one second that Ellie herself was actually sick, and had simply assumed it was Sabrina who had a cold. Ellie let the assumption stand, and said she'd probably be back at work tomorrow.

Then, once Sabrina was down for her morning nap, Dalton had asked her to pull up a chair beside his and help with his manuscript. Instead, she'd stood behind him. *Well* behind him. Putting a couple of feet of space between his back and her front, because—

Well, because in the last thirty-six hours everything between them had changed. Ever since he'd come close to kissing her—or she'd thought he had, she still wasn't sure if she'd read him right on that account—the equation that had seemed so balanced, had tipped to one side, and Ellie had yet to find a way to even it out again. She simply couldn't make A equal anything but confused.

"Unless you have X-ray vision, you can't read anything from way over there."

"I'm fine."

He swiveled around in his chair and tossed her a grin. "You seem anything but. In fact you seem uncomfortable. I do have another chair, you know. You could sit right next to me and make yourself at home." He pointed toward a second seat a few feet from where she stood.

"Speak for yourself. You don't seem so comfortable."

"Me? I'm just peachy."

She laughed. "What guy uses a word like that? Peachy?"

"Hey, I'm a writer. My vocabulary is wide and varied." Dalton turned back to his desk. He paged down in the computer, then pointed at the screen. "All right, stay there if you want. In this scene, the hero and the heroine are reunited for the first time in ten years. There are supposed to be all these emotions swirling in their heads, you know? That whole what-are-we-doing-here-together-again kind of thing, all the while there's a sense of danger in the background because they know the bad guy could be lurking around the corner."

"So there's still a lot of attraction brewing?"

"Yeah. And all those unanswered questions from their past." Dalton leaned back in his chair, unwittingly closing the distance between them, and ran a hand through his hair. "Except every time I try to show that, it comes out like they're a couple of guys talking about the Patriots' chances of making it to the Super Bowl again."

"Oh, it can't be that bad."

He waved at the screen. "Read it for yourself. You'll see. It has all the feeling of a punk rock song."

She stepped closer, peering over his shoulder and scanned the sentences. He was paying her to do that, after all, and she had agreed to offer her opinion. A few seconds later, she was forced to agree. "I'm no expert with emotions in books, because all I really have to go by is the romance novels I've read before, or at least the ones I used to have time to read," she said with a laugh. "Someday I hope to have time to read again."

"Kids get easier." Then he shrugged. "I hear. Not that I know myself, of course. Just my mom, you know, she had no free time for herself when we were little. But once we were up and ambulatory, and feeding ourselves, she had time to do stuff like read. And eat." He grinned.

"So there is hope for me to have a life." She echoed his smile and he met her gaze, held it for a long time. A tremor of connection ran through Ellie and she stepped back, allowing a bit of cold air to infiltrate the space. "Uh, you have the guy

more or less captured, I think. But the woman…
well, she's almost cardboard."

Dalton rose. He crossed to a bookshelf, and ran
his hand over a half dozen hardcover books with
his name running down the spine in bold letters.
"The critics have blasted me for this for years." He
shook his head and headed back to Ellie. "If I knew
how to write women, I'd be a bestseller. I did one
book right…and then seemed to lose my touch."

"Why?"

Her eyes were clear, guileless. She had no idea
what she was asking him, what wounds she was
opening up. "Because back with that first book, I
was pouring out a whole other story on the page.
I wasn't writing fiction so much as…" He let out
a breath and instead of speaking, reached up a
hand and cupped her jaw. Would she understand?
Would she know what he had gone through, how
he had torn his own heart out of his chest, slapped
it on a page and called it a book? And how, after
doing it once, he'd never been able to write
another book like that again?

Could Ellie, who had lost a loved one herself,
but in a different way, could she, of all people,
understand?

He held her, his fingers touching her, searching
for a connection, hoping for one. "Have you fallen
in love before, Ellie?"

Her mouth dropped open. The temptation to run his thumb along her lower lip, to taste what he had tasted before, roared inside Dalton. "Yes," she said, the word a whisper.

God, how he wanted to kiss her, taste her, feel her body against his. "And how did it feel?"

"Like…falling off a cliff, only with a cloud waiting at the bottom to catch you."

Poetry. She was poetry when she spoke. "And did he love you, too?"

She nodded, slow.

"If you met someone you loved again, after years and years apart, how would it feel? If say—" his gaze met hers, and a surge of electricity sparked in the air, as if lightning had hit the floor "—you and I had once been lovers and we were being reunited?"

"But we aren't."

Every ounce of him was watching her lips move, noting the way she inhaled, exhaled. For a second, he wanted to recapture those days when he wrote the first book, when he too used to believe in love. He wanted to feel what Ellie felt—to believe in poetry, in the clouds. "Pretend we are. Pretend you used to love me. How—" his thumb caressed the edge of her jaw, and her breath caught, held, along with his pulse "—would it feel to see me again? Would you be sad…or—"

now he did what he'd wanted to do ever since he'd met her, and traced the delicate skin along her lips "—excited?"

"Uh…" her breath escaped in a soft whoosh, "excited. But…uh, scared, too."

He leaned in closer. "Because?"

"Because you make me think about—"

Dalton waited, but she didn't finish the sentence. "Make you think about what?"

"About what I missed out on," she finished, the words a whisper, a sentence he wasn't sure she meant for him. She cast her lashes down for one long second, as if she was waiting, anticipating, hoping—

He'd kiss her.

A heartbeat passed between them. Another. Desire raged in Dalton's veins. When Ellie looked up at him again, his resistance nearly broke. Damn. What was he doing? How did it get to this point? How had they gone from nothing to an explosion like this in a matter of seconds?

"Thanks," he said, stepping back, breaking away, remembering who he was, why she was here, and most of all that she was a single mother who shouldn't get tangled up with an irascible writer with a cloudy personal history. "That was exactly what I needed."

Clouds of confusion marred her bright green

gaze, followed by a shadow of hurt. A shaky smile danced across her lips. "I'm…I'm glad."

"Yeah. Me, too." Dalton dropped into his chair and started typing, telling himself this was for the best. Getting involved with a package that came attached to a woman with a kid, all wrapped up with a white picket fence bow, would be a really bad idea.

A monumentally bad idea.

Instead, he poured everything he was feeling, every emotion churning in his gut, onto the page. He let those words flow from his heart to his fingers to the keyboard, the keystrokes flying as fast as hummingbirds, until the pages were filled.

The words, which had been as recalcitrant as mules in mud, flowed like a river now. Ellie hung back for a long time, just watching him write. He wasn't sure how to read her, so he just…didn't. He did what he did best, and ignored people, burying himself in his work.

Oh, she was an idiot.

Twice now, Ellie had thought Dalton was going to kiss her. This time, she'd even been so stupid as to close her eyes and wait.

And then what did he do? Say "thanks for the help" and sit down at his computer and start typing.

She smacked her forehead. What was she thinking? That a woman with a baby was some sex goddess/desire queen that a single guy would go ga-ga over?

Yeah, right.

Talk about completely misreading the signals. She'd been out of the dating scene so long, she might as well sign up for Dating for Dummies. Either way, it didn't matter.

The last thing she needed right now was a relationship. Heck, she didn't even have time for non-microwaveable meals, never mind men.

Okay, so she had made and eaten one homemade dinner this week. But that had only been because she felt sorry for Dalton. Based on what she'd found in his refrigerator, the man was clearly bordering on the edge of malnutrition.

She glanced at her watch. Fifteen, maybe twenty minutes before Sabrina would be awake. If she had any sense, she'd be using that time to work—not fret about a situation that would only complicate her life. A life that didn't need any more complications, that was for sure.

She headed downstairs and into his enormous great room, a two-story space filled with luxurious leather furniture, a massive stone gas log fireplace and hand-hewn mahogany tables. It had the density of manly furniture, but the comfort of a well-lived space. She could almost feel Dalton in this room, imagine him sitting on those sofas, sitting back against the soft, well-broken-in surfaces, watching a football game on a Monday night.

There she went again. Thinking about a man who wasn't even interested in her. She really needed to turn her brain off.

Ellie punched in the work number on her cell, and concentrated instead on her high-strung boss. Five minutes of conversation with Lincoln, and she had put Dalton out of her mind.

"Ellie, this isn't working. I can't have you out sick. When are you coming back? Are you feeling better? Tell me you are." Lincoln's voice rose with each syllable. "We've already had three meetings this morning. And I didn't have your input. It was a *disaster*."

"Three meetings?" She could only imagine how frustrated everyone at work was feeling. "I e-mailed detailed notes this morning, Lincoln. There shouldn't have been anything left on your agenda."

"We still had things to discuss. You have no idea how stressful this job is. How many details there are to cover."

Lincoln and his meetings. The man would have a meeting to talk about changing the toilet paper in the restrooms.

"Like what?"

"The format of the show, for one. I'm not sure I like the order we've come up with. Maybe we should shorten the intro by three seconds. It seems a little long. And move the soccer player up ahead of that piece on adoptions."

"Lincoln, the intro is fine. We've worked on it a hundred times. And if you shave three seconds from the intro, you have to reword the whole song. As for moving the soccer player, that will take away the incentive for people to hang on after the commercial break. You want people to sit through the commercials. The sponsors are the ones paying the tab."

Lincoln let out a huge sigh of relief. "See, this is what I needed to hear. You're always right, Ellie. You should be here, not at home. You are sick, aren't you?"

She let out a little cough, feeling bad for faking an illness, but knowing if she told the truth—that she'd opted for a day off so she could spend some time with her daughter and help out Dalton—Lincoln would make her come in to work. "Of course."

"Well, tomorrow, I expect you to work two hours overtime. That'll make up for not being here today. We can go over the shows for the rest of the month and—"

"Lincoln, I can't stay two hours late. I have to find childcare and—"

"You will if you want to keep your job. I told

you when you took this position that it would be demanding, Ellie." He let out a chuckle. "What I really meant is that *I* would be demanding. You want this job, you need to put in the time."

She needed the job. Needed the income desperately. Finding another position would take time— time to scour the classifieds, time to apply, time to go on interviews. Ellie ran a hand through her hair. "I'll be there, Linc."

"Thanks, Ellie. I knew I could count on you." He hung up, a single man with a single drive for his show and his network, and no understanding at all that his employees might have a personal life outside Channel 77.

"Yeah, that's the problem," Ellie said into the silent phone. And the one big thing she wanted to change—and couldn't.

CHAPTER SEVEN

THE baby would not cooperate.

Ellie tried rocking her. Tried feeding her. Tried changing her wet diaper. And still Sabrina would not quit crying. Bri kept reaching out her arms, as if grasping at an invisible toy.

And then Ellie realized what Bri wanted, the same thing Ellie wanted and shouldn't have. "You know he's not going to be happy, Bri. I'm not supposed to interrupt him before ten. It's not his turn."

Sabrina just kept on crying. Ellie knew this mood. There would be no settling Sabrina down, not until she got what she wanted. And what she wanted right now, whether it was 9:45 or 10:00, was Dalton.

Ellie crossed to Dalton's office and knocked on the door. "Dalton? Can I come in?"

"If you must."

As soon as she opened the door, Sabrina wriggled forward.

"Someone wanted to see you. And she's not

going to be happy until she does. I've been trying everything to get her to stop crying, and apparently it's you she wants right now."

"Me." No question mark on the end.

"Yep. Can you hold her for just a minute? Then I'll get her out of your hair. I promise."

"Take the kid off your hands." Another non-question.

"Just for a minute," she reassured him.

"I guess I could." He rose and headed over to Ellie, his scowl as deep as the Grand Canyon.

Odd. Dalton had no issues with watching Sabrina. Pushing the stroller. Rocking the car seat. Handing her a pacifier, putting her on her blanket, even holding her bottle. But physically holding the child—

It was like pulling teeth every time she tried to put Bri in his arms. She didn't believe him for one second about the screaming/smelly thing. And it wasn't as if he didn't seem to like Sabrina. He just didn't like to hold her.

Maybe he was afraid he'd drop her. She knew lots of people felt that way when they first got around babies. "She won't break, you know," Ellie said, handing Sabrina to Dalton.

"I kind of figured that," he said. "Otherwise, she'd come with one of those care labels."

Bri stopped crying the second she landed in

Dalton's arms, and twisted around, trying to fit into the space between his arms and his chest. Dalton, though, kept his distance, managing to keep her from slipping in too tightly.

"She really likes to snuggle," Ellie said.

"Yeah, I get that."

Okay, so maybe he wasn't a baby kind of guy. Except…she suspected he really was at heart. She'd caught him smiling at Sabrina a few times, even joking with her. Ellie backed up a few steps, purposely putting some distance between them. "Uh…" He made a face. "I think she just…"

Ellie grinned. "You're holding her. Baby rules."

"You did that on purpose."

Ellie laughed. "Honest, I didn't. But those *are* the baby rules. The one holding the kid when the diaper gets dirtied, has to change it."

"So not fair." He held the baby toward her. "She's yours. You change her."

Ellie crossed her arms over her chest, grinning as she stepped further back. "No."

"My sisters used to try to trap me this way," he said, crossing the room to Ellie in three quick strides. Before she could move away, he'd grabbed one of her arms. "I amended the baby rules."

"Amended?"

"Yeah. If I tag you, you have to help." His blue eyes met hers. "Tag."

She laughed. "All right, I'll help. But I call the top end."

"Oh, you play dirty." He chuckled. "I like that, even if I'm losing."

Five minutes later, they had Sabrina on the floor, lying on a plastic mat. A package of wipes and a new diaper lay beside her. Dalton was on his knees, scowling. "I would never do this for anyone else," he said to her.

Ellie readied a wipe. "Trust me, if she wasn't my kid, I wouldn't do it, either."

"Hold your breath. I'm going in." He undid the tape on the sides, and dropped the front of the diaper, and his scowl deepened.

Ellie couldn't help but laugh some more. Dalton looked up and met her gaze, and echoed her laughter. She handed him the wipe, then another, and another. In a few minutes, they had the baby's diaper changed and their hands cleaned. "Was that so bad?"

"Was it so good?"

"It was for Bri."

He looked down at the baby. "Well, as long as it was good for her."

"After coming from a big family," Ellie said, watching him and the baby, building a sort of rapport dance, "did you ever want to have kids of your own?"

The question seemed to slam into him like a brick wall. Dalton handed Sabrina back to Ellie, that glacier from the park back in an instant. "I think she wants you now. I have to go back to work." He spun on his heel and disappeared back upstairs.

Conversation over.

Sabrina looked at Ellie, as if her mother would have an explanation for Dalton's mysterious behavior, but Ellie was just as mystified as the baby. Ellie knew one thing for sure—this wasn't about Sabrina. It was about something that had happened to Dalton. Something he didn't want to talk about.

Apparently, the emotional blocks weren't just in his books.

Sabrina slept in the playpen, her belly full. Night had fallen, its thick blanket covering the neighborhood with dark ebony. Everyone in the little corner around Dalton and Ellie had gone to bed.

Except Dalton and Ellie.

In Dalton's house, a single light burned on the second floor, where he and Ellie stayed in his office, neither of them aware of the hours that had passed while they worked. Once the baby had fallen asleep, the two of them had dropped into a natural rhythm with the book, as he talked out a scene, she gave him input, he wrote, then printed off the pages for her to read and critique. He'd put in the changes, then they'd start the process all over again.

"Oh my goodness," Ellie said, "look at the time."

Dalton glanced at his computer clock. "It's one-thirty in the morning. I'm sorry. I didn't expect us to keep working this late."

"That's okay. It was fun."

He chuckled. "Writing? Fun?"

"Well, sure. Don't you ever have fun doing this?"

He leaned back and stretched. "I guess I used to, in the beginning. But I haven't thought about it being fun for a long time." Then his gaze met hers, and something exchanged between them, like a rope uncoiling, then twisting up again. "But tonight, yeah, it was fun."

She smiled, one of the dozens of different smiles Ellie had that Dalton didn't think he could begin to describe. "Worth the late night?"

"Yeah."

"I know I'll be paying for it tomorrow."

"I'm sure you'll make me pay, too." He grinned. "Baby rules."

"Oh, yeah, those will apply. In spades."

How long had it been since he'd flirted like this with a woman? Had fun…off the page? Way too long, that was for sure.

"I should get going," Ellie said, sending a shiver

of disappointment through Dalton. Regardless of the time, he didn't want this moment to end. "But I wanted to mention one more thing before I left."

"Shoot." About him? Or the book?

"I don't know if you want to add this or not," she paused, "but if I were her…"

"What? Go ahead, I can take the criticism. But be gentle. I've got a tender ego."

She snorted. "Yeah. And I'm a Sumo wrestler underneath all this." She flexed her biceps, grinning. "Well, what I thought you should add, is your heroine thinking that he probably doesn't feel the same way."

"What do you mean?"

"In that section there?" She leaned past him, to point at a paragraph at the top of the page. "She watches him walk away, and I think it hurts her because she feels one thing and your hero feels another. Or maybe he doesn't, because the reader doesn't read his feelings in this chapter. All you have is hers."

"And you think I need to add her interpretation of how he feels."

Ellie nodded. Her clear green gaze met his. "Because you know men and they're not so good at spelling out what they're thinking."

"No, they're not. Keep their cards close to their vest."

"But if he told her, she'd be able to react." Again, her gaze held his. Asking a question? Or just offering input?

All Dalton had to do was ask a few questions and he could be right back there, playing with fire again. The same fire he'd managed to avoid earlier, when he'd stopped that kiss before it started.

Don't ask.

Let it go.

Move on.

He leaned back in his chair, one arm draped over the back, and studied her. "What would she be reacting to?" He never had been good at walking away from a pile of matches and some very beautiful kindling.

"Depends on what he tells her," Ellie said.

She was asking him if he was interested. He could tell. By the way she was watching him, and not at all looking at the book. Asking if he'd walked away from kissing her because he didn't like her—or because he did and he was trying to be a nice guy.

"Because up until now, he hasn't told her much of anything, has he?" Dalton said.

"No." The word came out as a breath.

"Maybe he just didn't know what to say." He held her gaze. "Or maybe he didn't want to change the rules of the game."

"Something sure changed, Dalton," Ellie said, gesturing to the pages he'd just rewritten, "because five minutes ago, your heroine was a blue-eyed blonde. Now she's a green-eyed brunette. Sound like anyone you know?"

What was he thinking? How had that happened? "I…" His voice trailed off. He didn't have an answer.

Ellie rose and headed for the door. "Maybe both of us need to get our heads out of the fictional world. Because what happens there isn't real. I'm a single mom, Dalton, and if there's one thing I've got in abundance, it's reality. And that means I don't have time to turn the next hundred pages to find out how someone feels."

Then she was gone, leaving Dalton with the imaginary people in his fictional book, who were just as conflicted as him.

Lunch time.

Dalton hadn't dreaded a meal like this in… forever. He'd have skipped lunch altogether, if Ellie hadn't gone and made chili, unwittingly concocting his all-time favorite meal. He'd caught a whiff of the spicy concoction from his office, and been unable to resist the lure of both the beef dish and his rumbling stomach.

She sat at the table, the baby cradled in one arm,

a bottle propped in its mouth. A bowl of chili sat before Ellie, steam curling upward. A second sat at his place, flanked by two pieces of cornbread.

Cornbread, too? Oh, he was a goner. There'd be no resisting now for sure. "You treat me too well."

She smiled, and the sun seemed to rise on her face. If there was one trait about Ellie that he liked, it was that she forgave easily. The tension from last night was gone, and she was back to her usual happy self. "Actually, I should be thanking you. With the time off from work, I finally have the opportunity to indulge one of my passions."

The word brought back the memory of nearly kissing her. And the urge to finish the job. "Oh, yeah? What's that?" he asked, hoping she'd mention the very thing he was thinking of.

"Cooking. I love to cook. I never get time because when I get home from work, I've got to feed Sabrina, give her a bath, get her ready for bed, and by then I'm exhausted. Plus, what's the point when…" Her voice trailed off.

"When what?"

She shrugged. "When I'm only cooking for one?"

"Well, anytime you get the urge to indulge—" he wanted to say any of your passions, but he stopped himself "—your need to cook, you know where I live, and you know I probably ate junk food all day. My stomach is yours, milady."

She smiled again, and his heart skipped a beat. For just a second, Dalton couldn't remember why he had ever thought getting involved with Ellie Miller was a bad idea.

Then his gaze dropped to the baby in her lap, sucking greedily at the bottle, and he remembered why. Her reality. One he didn't want or need to be a part of.

He dipped into the chili, and swallowed the bite. "This is terrific. You should have been a chef."

"My mother taught me to cook. It was how we spent our Saturdays."

"Is your mother still alive?"

Ellie shook her head. "My dad lives in Florida, but Mom died a few years ago. Where are your parents?"

"Living a comfortable, and might I add, well deserved retirement, in Arizona. Three of my sisters are there, too, with their expansive brood of children, so my parents are surrounded by grandchildren."

This was easy conversation, the kind he could handle. Not that Dalton, of course, regularly talked about his family, or heck, much of anything with anyone. It just went to show him how hermit-like his life had become. Ever since he'd sold his first book ten years ago, he'd retreated more and more into that writer show, withdrawing from social life under the guise of deadlines and brainstorming.

Now, though, sitting with Ellie, discussing the most basic of things—where he came from—was as enjoyable as the chili.

"And the rest of your siblings?" Ellie asked.

"One sister is unmarried and traveling the globe, backpacking in the Sierras and tackling world peace one country at a time. One of my brothers is just finishing up his PhD, then he's supposed to get married at the end of the year. Peter, the oldest and the one who settled down first, lives here in Boston with his wife and three kids." Dalton thought for a second, doing the mental math on who he'd left out. "I've got another brother who lives in California with his wife, and they're expecting their first kid sometime in the next month. Two sisters married guys who are best friends and they all live on a cul-de-sac in New Jersey. It's like a little suburban soap opera. And my two youngest sisters, both of them are in an engineering or electrical or some such technical kind of job, are not married yet, but my mother drops hints on a daily basis and has sent out the word among the retirement community, looking for any eligible grandsons."

Ellie laughed. "That's a lot to keep track of. I've never been so glad to be an only child."

"You should try it at Christmas. When all of us are together, it's a zoo. And I mean that literally."

"Must be fun."

He found himself smiling. For all the chaos, all the insanity, his family had a lot of plusses. "It was. Don't tell my brothers and sisters, but I miss them when they're not around."

"Are you all pretty close?"

"Enough that they can tell me how to run my life." A sardonic grin filled his face.

Ellie let out a little laugh. "Believe me, it doesn't matter what size your family is, someone always has an opinion. My dad gives me advice all the time. He thinks…"

When she didn't finish, he waved her on. "He thinks what?"

"He thinks I should move on." She picked at her food, then sat back against the chair. "That it's been long enough, and I should think about a life for me. A love life, specifically."

"And what do you think about that advice?"

"I think if my dad wants to give me a live-in nanny for Christmas, then I'll take his advice." She grinned.

But beneath the smile, Dalton could see—

What could he see? At first, he thought he saw resistance, a stubbornness, the same recalcitrant streak that ran through him, that made him want to run the other way whenever anyone tried to tell him what to do. But no, it was more than that. It was—

Longing.

And as he peeled back the layers and unearthed

that emotion, he heard the stirrings of the same feeling in his own heart, too. He rose, grabbing his bowl, even though it was still half-full, and headed for the stove. Staying busy topping off the chili, and grabbing more cornbread kept him from connecting with Ellie.

From letting her see the reflection of her emotions in his eyes.

"This is great chili."

She grinned. "You already said that. Are you avoiding the conversation, Dalton Scott?" Ellie flipped the baby onto her shoulder, and started patting her back.

"Of course not. Just had to tell you how good the food is on the second helping. Actually, twice as good."

"Uh-huh." Sabrina let out a burp. "Apparently, the formula is not too bad around here, either." She glanced over at her daughter, and the soft smile—the one reserved solely for the baby—stole slowly across Ellie's face.

Dalton's gut clenched. He stopped eating, and just watched Ellie, as transfixed as if he had been glued to his chair. She leaned over, pressed a soft kiss to Sabrina's nearly bald forehead, then inched out of her chair and put her down inside the portable playpen.

"Wait," Dalton whispered.

Ellie pivoted. "Why?"

"Maybe we should set that up in the spare bedroom. She'll probably sleep better in there. Less distractions. You know, while we're getting the dishes done and everything."

She grinned. "You do dishes?" she said, her voice also at a whisper.

Dalton crossed to her, still mesmerized by the softness in her face, the way her smile seemed to light every feature, brighten the green in her eyes. His heart hammered in his chest, lungs holding every breath hostage.

"I'm pretty handy around a house," he said quietly, so close he could have kissed her without any effort.

"That's…that's good to know," she whispered, turning her face toward his, which brought her lips just under his, a whisper from kissing. Ellie's breath caught, her chest heaving.

His gaze fixed on her pulse ticking in her throat, the heat emanating between them. Then he reached out, his hand straying to her waist, lingering for one long second. Desire beat a steady drum in Dalton's veins. How he wanted to haul her to him, to quench this thirst. To kiss Ellie until neither one of them had anything left.

"You wanted to know something last night," he said.

"I did?"

"How I felt." He watched her mouth open, then close, then open again, lips parted slightly, just enough to tease and tempt him. "*This* is how I feel, Ellie, every time I look at you." With a groan, Dalton leaned in and kissed her, drawing in the sweet, floral notes of her perfume as he did.

She melted into his arms, as if she, too, had lost the battle against willpower. Dalton's fingers tangled in Ellie's hair, urging her closer, wanting her to fill the holes inside him, holes that ran so deep, so dark, he couldn't see his way to the bottom.

Ellie tasted like Dalton had always imagined goodness would taste. Sweet, almost like home-made cookies. So wonderful, so soft and perfect, desire ran through him at a breakneck pace, urging him to take this another step, to do more, to take this beyond a kitchen and a kiss. Then the baby stirred, bringing Dalton back to reality, and away from Ellie. "We should get that set up, so the kid can nap."

"Uh…yeah." Ellie turned away, and picked up the baby. Dalton gathered up the playpen. As he did, he caught the scent of Ellie's perfume, the sweet floral and fruity notes lingering in the air of his house as if she'd put her personal stamp on every wall.

A day ago, two days, he'd have been annoyed. But today, well, he didn't feel as upset by that thought.

The problem?

Just the fact that he was getting used to the idea of a woman in his house—a woman with a baby—was a clear sign he was in too deep. He needed to remember his priorities. Remember that he wasn't the kind of guy cut out for settling down and making families.

And if anyone was looking for a father to complete her perfect little image, it was Ellie Miller.

Once Sabrina was settled and asleep, Ellie headed back to the kitchen, sure Dalton would be gone. She expected him to hole back up in his office—promise to do dishes or no promise.

But no, he was waiting. He had the chili already put away, and was in the process of wrapping the cornbread in plastic wrap. The earlier sexual tension had diffused with the time apart. Ellie told herself she was glad, but a part of her wished they could rewind the clock and finish what they had started with that kiss, so she could finally quiet this constant ache.

"It's about time," Dalton said with a grin. "I thought you abandoned me."

"It took a while to get Sabrina to settle down. She woke up when I put her down, so I had to pat her back until she fell asleep again. I wasn't going to miss out on that afternoon nap." Ellie picked up the dishes from the kitchen table and loaded them into the sink.

"You go sit. I'll get it. Between work and the kid, it's pretty clear your day is hard enough. And, you cooked lunch." He gestured toward the machine under the counter. "Not to mention, I have a dishwasher that will do that job."

"I don't mind doing dishes. It relaxes me."

He shook his head. "There is something inherently wrong with that statement. Especially when modern technology is here to take away the burden."

She grinned. "Taking the easy way out? I thought you said you do dishes."

"I do." He popped open the dishwasher. "In here."

"Wimpy, wimpy. A real man would wash them, with me."

"A real man, huh? Is that a challenge I hear in your voice?"

"Are you taking me up on it?"

He put the chili and cornbread in the refrigerator, then shut the door and pivoted back to Ellie. Dalton considered her, a grin swinging across his face, lighting up his eyes. The stir of desire awakened anew in Ellie's gut—heck, who was she kidding, it had never died down from earlier when he'd kissed her.

"A pretty woman daring me to wash dishes,"

Dalton said, pushing off from the fridge to join her at the sink. "Now what man in his right mind would turn that down?"

She handed him a dish towel, and wondered if she really wanted help with the dishes, or if she just wanted to open up a whole new can of worms. "Not one who wants another meal, that's for sure."

He chuckled. "I have to work for my supper, is that it?"

"It certainly helps you to get on my good side. Especially with dinner just a few hours around the corner."

"And what's for dinner?"

"Depends on how good of a job you do here."

"Oh, I'll do a good job, Ellie. You can count on that." Temptation and anticipation coiled tight in Ellie's gut as Dalton slid in on the left of her. She was playing with fire, and not just a couple of matches and some kindling, either, but a full-out four-alarmer. What was she thinking?

That was the trouble. She wasn't thinking.

She filled the sink with hot soapy water. As she did, Dalton leaned against the counter, seeming to exude sex appeal. Ellie had to remember to breathe. To keep her eyes on the job at hand so she didn't crack a glass or shatter a bowl. She ran a sponge around the rim of a bowl, then rinsed it, before handing the dish to Dalton. "Make yourself useful," she teased.

"Yes, ma'am." He dried the bowl, then moved behind her, so close he nearly brushed up against her. "Uh, excuse me, but this goes right into this cabinet. Right here."

The temptation fire blazed out of control. And Ellie wasn't doing a thing to get it back under control. She just kept washing dishes, and handing them to Dalton. Enjoying every second of this game.

What would it be like if she lived with Dalton? If they did this every night? If he…

Touched her? Took her in his arms and did more than just kiss her? If, after all this, he took her upstairs and made love to her?

She had been alone for so long, and right now, this felt so much like being married, and the tension boiling between them was both unbearable and sweet at the same time. It had started that first day, quadrupling every time they were alone together.

He dried the glass in his hand and put it in the cabinet to the right of her, doing the same slide across, sending Ellie's nerve endings pinging. "Maybe we should dirty more dishes."

"How's a seven-course dinner sound?"

"I was hoping for eight."

Ellie laughed. Damn. It felt really, really good to laugh. To flirt with a man. To have him flirt back. She handed Dalton another bowl, a second glass. Heat ignited in the space between them, rising with each second.

A moment later, she had handed him the last pot, then pulled the drain. "That's it."

She turned, putting her back to the counter. Dalton moved in front of her, placing his hands on either side. Ellie drew in a breath and held it, losing herself in the deep blue of his eyes. "What are we doing here?"

"I can tell you what we're not doing," he said. "The dishes. We finished those."

"You know what I mean, Dalton." How she wanted to forget her responsibilities. Forget her life. But she was a single mother, and she might be able to pretend for a minute or two that she didn't have a baby sleeping in the bedroom upstairs—

But that was as long as she could live that façade. A minute. Because Sabrina was upstairs, expecting her mother to be responsible, every single minute of every single day.

And being responsible meant not getting wrapped up in a man who had no intentions of making any of these kisses permanent.

"I can't play at a relationship. I have to think of Sabrina."

"You want it all."

"I have a daughter, Dalton. We're a package

deal." She smiled, knowing her life had changed in more ways than one the day Sabrina had been born.

"If you're looking for the kind of man who can be a boyfriend to you, and a father to Sabrina, I'm sorry," he said. "But that's not me. Despite what we've been doing here for the last couple of days, I'm just not father material." He backed up, inserting distance that became as cold as an Arctic wind. "And I don't think I ever will be."

CHAPTER EIGHT

SABRINA looked terrified. It had to be the purple spiked hair and the nose piercings. Three of them, to be exact.

Ellie sat in the living room of her house on Wednesday night, interviewing her fourth babysitter, all of them recommended by a local college, and thought the future had never looked so bleak.

She couldn't work with Dalton anymore. He came with too many complications. Mrs. Winterberry would be gone for an indefinite period of time. And if the last few babysitters she'd interviewed had been any indication, there wasn't a single affordable childcare option available in the greater Boston area, at least not in the immediate future.

She could try daycare—and be left with oh, fifty-seven cents at the end of her paycheck. Or try working from home, and risk losing her job, after Lincoln noticed she hadn't come into the office in days.

Ellie closed the door after the spike-haired girl left and dropped onto the floor beside Sabrina, who lay on her back on her blanket, blowing bubbles at the ceiling. "Well, kiddo, we have a problem."

Sabrina turned her head at the sound of her mother's voice and smiled, cooing gently.

"I can't take you to work, I can't stay home, and I can't bring you to Dalton's anymore. It's just too…hard to be around him and not…well, not kiss him. It's not that I don't want to kiss him, because I do. All the time. *That's* the problem."

"Unh, Unh." Sabrina rolled to her side, her little chubby fists reaching out for her mother.

Ellie picked her up and held her to her chest. Sabrina didn't squirm, simply settled into place. Clearly, all the time Ellie had spent with her daughter lately had had a positive effect. "The trouble is, I miss him. Even though I know he's totally the wrong man for me." She glanced down at her little girl. "And I think you miss him, too."

Sabrina's big blue eyes seemed to agree.

The problem was much bigger than Ellie had thought. Because there were now two Miller girls who were falling for Dalton Scott—and he'd already made it clear that he wasn't the right man for either one of them.

* * *

Dalton paced his office. Paced his living room. Paced his kitchen.

And still couldn't work off the nervous energy that coiled so tight inside him, he felt like a spring ready to explode.

He missed Ellie, damn it. He knew she was there, just across the street, and he could have her in his arms again, if only—

If only he could give her the one thing she wanted. And deserved.

A family. A husband.

Impossible. He was a master at writing impossible situations, the kind his readers thought the hero could never solve, and then at the eleventh hour, some miracle solution would come along, or the hero would find the bad guy just before he got away for the last time. But that was fiction, and this was real life. In Dalton's non-fiction world, there was no miracle coming along to provide the answers he needed, one that would allow him to have Ellie in his life, without him having to make the commitment she needed—and deserved.

But he needed to find a way to have her here. A way that worked for both of them. Not just because she'd been so helpful with the book, but because Ellie had brought a calming presence to his days that Dalton hadn't had in years.

A calm, and a chaos, like two sides of the same

coin, all at once. Between the picnics and the dinners, and the diaper changes and the crying baby, he'd found something new and unexpected, that left a cavernous hole in his house the minute she walked out the door.

"You gonna live?" Peter sat in Dalton's favorite armchair, sipping a beer this time, and watching his younger brother with an amused expression on his face.

"I'm fine."

"Yeah, you look just fine. About as *fine* as a tiger kept in a cat cage." Peter gestured out the window. "And I bet that woman from across the street is the whole reason you're working that carpet into dust."

"I'm worried about my career. The book isn't going well."

"The books haven't been going well for the past couple of years, and I've never seen you this worked up about any of them before."

"Yeah, well, this time my career is on the line."

Concern etched lines across Peter's face. "Really? How so?"

Dalton stopped pacing and lowered himself onto the hearth. He propped his arms across his knees. "My editor said this is the do or die book. Either this one comes in and really knocks his socks off, or I better find a real job."

"You'll do fine, Dalton. You always do."

"I don't, Pete. Not since the first book." The blockbuster that had made Dalton Scott a household name. And set an impossible standard he'd never been able to reach again.

"What's he say you're doing wrong? Maybe I can help."

Dalton let out a short laugh. "I don't think so. Reuben said it's the women in my books. I'm just not getting the…well, the emotion in there."

Peter took a long gulp of beer and arched a brow.

"What? I know you have something to say to that."

His brother raised and dropped one shoulder. "You know exactly why you're not getting the emotion in there."

"If I knew, Pete, I'd have fixed the problem a long time ago."

Peter put his beer bottle on the end table, laying it carefully on a coaster—apparently a learned behavior because Dalton had never seen him do such a thing when they'd lived at home—and then sat back, arms crossed over his chest. "I've learned a thing or two, in the seven years I've been married, Dalton. And the biggest is that you can't shut yourself off to a woman. You do that, and you'll never go anywhere in a relationship."

"I'm not looking to go anywhere in a relationship. I just want to finish my book and deliver what my editor wants."

"And he wants emotion, right?"

Dalton nodded.

Peter leaned forward, his older, wiser and more experienced gaze connecting with Dalton's. "Then tell me the last time you connected with a woman. Really connected. In here." He patted his heart. "That's where the emotion is, little brother. Until you do that, you won't be finding any emotion to put on your page, or in your life."

Dalton scowled and got to his feet. "You don't know what you're talking about. You're not a writer."

"Maybe not. But I am a man. One who's been married a long time. And if you ask me, it all works the same." Peter got to his feet, then clasped Dalton on the shoulder. "You've let one mistake control you for too long. You need to forgive yourself. Then you can move on. And have the life you deserve."

"I have forgiven myself."

"Have you?" Peter asked. Then he glanced out the window, at Ellie, who was crossing the street, Sabrina on her shoulder. "I hope you have, because I see opportunity about to knock. And I'd hate for you to miss it, little brother."

* * *

Ellie had no idea what she was doing here. She'd been perfectly content at home, with Sabrina. Almost set, in fact, to get both of them ready for bed.

After the babysitter debacle, though, she'd realized she was stuck and in no better of a position with her daycare situation than she had been when Mrs. Winterberry had called her Monday morning. She had no childcare options for tomorrow, a handful of precious sick days left, that she needed to save for when Sabrina had an ear infection or a cold, and no other choices left.

Except for Dalton. Back to square one.

Before she pressed the doorbell, she made some decisions. She'd lay down some ground rules—the same ones she had tried to lay down before, until she had gotten distracted by his blue eyes. Well, there'd be no more of that. From now on, they'd steer clear of each other. There'd be strict drop-offs and pick-ups. No being alone with him. And no kissing whatsoever. This would be a clear-cut employment relationship.

She'd make sure of that by paying him, which was why she had brought her checkbook.

Ellie rang the bell, and the door opened. "I will not kiss you and I won't—"

"Glad to hear that. My wife wouldn't like it." A man who looked a lot like Dalton, only in an older version, gave her a grin, then stuck out his hand. "Dalton's older brother, Peter. You must be Ellie, from across the street."

Her face heated, and she was sure, turned five different shades of crimson. "I'm so sorry. I had this big speech planned and it just sort of exploded when the door opened."

"That's okay. It seems to be the day to tell Dalton what to do." He chuckled, then gestured for her to enter. "Go easy on him. I already read him the riot act." With a wave, Peter headed down the stairs and got into his minivan.

Ellie crossed the threshold and into Dalton's house. Surprise lit his features when he saw her, sending a little rocket of joy through her.

"Hi. I didn't expect to see you again today."

"I, uh, ran into a snag on the babysitter thing. I thought I could hire one of those college girls I was interviewing tonight, but it turns out most of them were sent over from the FBI's ten most wanted list."

Dalton laughed. "Not the best candidates?"

"I wouldn't let them watch my goldfish, never mind my daughter." She shifted Sabrina to the opposite shoulder. When she did, the baby's attention swiveled toward Dalton, her big blue eyes as rapt on him as they usually were on her bottle.

"So you're here to take the lesser of two evils?" He grinned.

As much as she didn't want to be tempted,

didn't want to fall under his spell again, an echoing smile curved across her face. "Something like that." She cleared her throat, reminded herself what she'd come here to say. If she didn't get it out now, she never would. And then where would they be? Right back in each other's arms. That might feel very, very good, but it would be a very, very bad idea. "Before we get wrapped up in this arrangement again, I'd like to lay down a few rules."

He nodded, somber, as if he'd anticipated this. "For a serious conversation, we need serious food. Come on, let's have some coffee. And cake."

"Cake? You baked?"

"Not me. Peter's wife. I think she thinks I'm at risk of starving to death because I live alone. She's always sending something over here. Tonight, it was black forest cheesecake."

Chocolate and cheesecake. Ellie's stomach rumbled. It was as if someone had opened up her head and read not just her mind, but her hormones.

"I was craving that exact thing," Ellie said as she followed him into the kitchen. "You'll have to bring me to the family reunion so I can thank her properly for reading my mind."

They were innocent words, meant only as a joke, Dalton was sure, but taken in another way, they implied a future. Days, weeks, months past this babysitting gig.

A future he used to think about having, back before he'd made that mistake with Julia. Dalton pushed away the thoughts and paused by the coffeepot, his hand resting on the silver machine. "Uh, coffee?"

"Sure. Decaf, though, or I'll be awake when I should be sleeping." She patted the baby's bottom with one hand, and masked a yawn with the other. "With her, I need every hour I can get. Especially after the last few days. Geez, there are times when it seems like I can't sleep enough."

"Decaf it is." Dalton got busy filling the pot, while Ellie made herself at home in his kitchen, withdrawing plates from the cabinet and forks from the drawer. Every few seconds, he glanced over at Ellie, noticing how natural it had become, in a matter of days, to have her here. She had simply become a part of his home.

Dalton's home, of all places. He was the hermit, the man who kept to himself, who holed up in his office and limited his interaction with others to the people he created on the page. Now he had a woman in his kitchen with a baby on her hip, and he was growing used to having them around.

He wasn't sure if that was a good thing or a bad thing, because getting used to having her here also meant getting used to being part of this trio of a family—and that was definitely not something on Dalton's life agenda.

He knew better than to attempt *that* again.

Ellie put the dishes on the table, then pulled a long skinny knife from the center drawer. "What's that?" Dalton asked.

"A cake knife."

"A what?"

She laughed. "A cake knife. Didn't you know you had one?"

"I don't know half the stuff I have in this kitchen. My mother and sisters gave me all this stuff, like one of those take-pity-on-the-bachelor gift parties. Except for the bologna, of course."

"What you need is a woman," she said, then her face colored. "Forget I said that." She shook her head, and covered for another yawn.

"Here, let me take her," he said, reaching for the kid. Not because he had some overwhelming urge to hold the kid or anything, but because he wanted to change the subject. "You look like your arm's about to break."

"Thanks," Ellie said, handing over the baby. "Don't let her fall asleep on you, though, or I'll pay the price later."

"Not being mean," Dalton said, "but you look like you already are falling asleep. You're exhausted. Go sit down on the couch. Let me take care of you for a change." He took the cake knife, sliced the cake and put the sliver onto the plate, then repeated for a second slice.

"I'm not tired." She yawned, then let out a half laugh. "Okay, maybe I am. But it comes with the territory. I can't remember the last time I had a full night's sleep."

"Then go sit," he said, handing her the slice of cake. "I'll finish brewing the coffee and bring you a cup when it's done."

"Are you sure?"

"Go." He waved her toward the living room. "Before I throw you out."

She laughed as she left the room, but her laughter didn't have its usual punch. He hadn't been kidding—she really did look exhausted. Undoubtedly, working a job, juggling the demands of the baby, and then going home and taking care of her own house drained Ellie. He couldn't imagine balancing all she did by himself. Heck, he couldn't imagine juggling it all with himself and a clone.

"Just you and me now, kid. You okay with that?" He bounced the baby lightly against his hip, then crossed to the cabinet and got out two coffee mugs. He'd gotten used to holding the kid over the last few days, which alone told him he was in too deep. Told him he was getting too close.

Sabrina grasped at his shirt, clutching the cotton of his T-shirt in her fist, as if she were holding on for dear life.

"No coffee for you. Sorry."

Beneath his grasp, the kid felt soft and fuzzy, in her peach and white pajamas. She snuggled in against him, as if she'd found her sweet spot here, and she wasn't going anywhere.

It felt…nice. Almost like she belonged there. She'd started to grow on him, this nearly twenty pound bundle of poo and puke. For a kid, she didn't make a lot of noise, and she had a tendency to pay attention to everything. Right now, she was staring at him, her eyes wide and inquisitive. Dalton stared back, thinking he'd never seen eyes such a light color of blue before. Her gaze had a hint of her mother's green, which made him wonder if the blue would yield to the maternal shade. Either way, her eyes would still be pretty.

"What are you looking at?" he asked.

She kept staring. Like she was waiting for him to do something.

He was tempted to put her down. Back in the car seat or the playpen, or even down on the carpet to crawl to her heart's content. But something kept him holding tight to the baby. Maybe it was the way she was gripping his shirt, or the way she kept looking at him, as if she wanted to—

Play.

He racked his brain, trying to think of a game, one that a kid her age could play with him. Then he remembered one his mother had played a thousand times with the little kids. Dalton picked up a dish towel from the countertop, put the cloth in front of his eyes, then dropped it down again. "Boo."

And just like that…the kid laughed, the sound pouring from her like bubbles breaking over rocks. Her whole body shook, belly rolling like jelly.

Awe struck Dalton, hit him as hard as a bolt of lightning. He stared at the kid for a long second, just drawing in the sound. "You liked that, huh?" Who knew he, of all people, could make a kid laugh like that? He'd always stayed away from engaging with kids. He'd done the bare minimum, then gotten the heck out of Dodge. And now, here was this kid, laughing like heck. Dalton chuckled, then raised the towel again, holding it a fraction longer this time. "Uh…uh…boo!"

An explosion of giggles poured out of Sabrina and she bounced up and down on his arm, as if begging him to do it again.

Holy cow. The kid stared at him, anticipation widening her eyes, dropping her jaw. He could almost imagine that she…

Liked him.

The realization socked him deep. For a second,

Dalton didn't know what to do, or say. He held her, looking into those big baby blues, and feeling that he had crossed a major threshold, one he hadn't been sure he wanted to cross, had been afraid to traverse.

Then found it wasn't so bad after all.

Sabrina bounced some more. "Unh-unh." She wanted him to keep going. She wanted him…to keep playing.

She really did like him. Dalton swallowed, and held onto the feeling for a moment, turning it this way and that, then found a smile curving across his face, and a light burst of joy rising in his chest.

"Well, kid, if I'd known it was this easy to keep you happy, I'd have grabbed a towel the first day." He slid it up a third time, this time in front of the kid's eyes, laughing as he did, anticipation pooling inside him as much as her. "Oh-oh. Where'd you go? You hiding on me? Ah…Boo!"

She loved that one even more. Sabrina bounced so hard, Dalton had to grab onto her with his other arm before she sprang so far, she fell on the floor. "Easy there, cowgirl."

She stared at him, her mouth open, waiting. He could see the expectation in every line of her face, hoping he'd do that magical thing all over again.

And so he obliged. Again and again, so many times, he lost track of the time, forgetting the cake and the coffee, and everything, for a long, long time. All he heard was the steady stream of giggles pouring from Sabrina like a waterfall of miracles. He found himself laughing, letting go, getting completely wrapped up in the moment and loving every second of it. Beginning to love…

Her.

And that was so not him. But it was a new side of himself that he found he enjoyed. Liked, even. If you'd asked Dalton five minutes earlier if he thought he could ever get a baby to laugh like that, he'd have said no, never. But here he was, doing the one thing he tried never to—holding a baby tight—and she was delighting in him and a silly dish towel like he was the funniest comedian to come along since Bob Hope.

Something grew in his heart and took flight with every "boo" and giggle. Something light, something Dalton couldn't quantify. Something a lot like Ellie's clouds. Dalton didn't know quite what to do with that emotion so he set it aside. Deal with it later, he told himself.

A part of him, though, wanted to capture this feeling and hold it tight. To hold onto it for the days ahead when Ellie and Sabrina would be back in their house across the street and he would be here again in his. Alone.

When the towel's charm finally wore off, Dalton

dropped it back onto the counter, and patted Sabrina's back. "If you liked that, wait till you see how funny I can be with a clothespin on my nose."

"Ba-ba-ba," Sabrina said, her voice winding down with each syllable. She watched him a little longer, then did something she had never done before.

She laid her head on his chest.

Dalton froze.

Sabrina stayed where she was, her soft cheek against his heart, her warm body pressed to his. One fist opened and closed on his T-shirt, while the other hand held tight to his waist. She let out a little high-pitched sigh of contentment. Her head lay against his heart, rising and falling with his breaths.

For a long time, Dalton stood right where he was, holding the baby, not sure whether to move or breathe. The coffeepot finished its cycle with a final gurgle, the glub-glub popping Dalton out of his stupor. "Hey, kid," he said, thinking that would get the baby to move.

But she only snuggled closer.

He turned to talk to her again, to tell her he was no one she wanted to get comfy on, but when he did, he caught a whiff of her shampoo. A sweet, fresh scent, with a touch of something he thought was called chamomile.

Beneath his nose, her hair was as soft as

feathers, tickling lightly against his skin. He paused, inhaling the baby-light scent, allowing himself that one second of pretending.

Pretending she was his. That he was Sabrina's father. He trailed a finger along the peachy soft skin of her cheek, the fantasy of this being his family, his life, continuing. He nuzzled Sabrina's soft head, and imagined carrying her upstairs, putting his daughter to bed, and then shutting the door. To cross the hall and join Ellie, and together he and Ellie would—

Dalton drew back. He filled one of the coffee mugs and headed out of the kitchen, before those thoughts could get too deeply ingrained. They could never become reality, so there was no sense thinking them. He'd hand the kid back to Ellie, and be done with it.

But when he reached the living room, he realized it wouldn't be that easy. Because Ellie had fallen asleep on his couch, her face soft and stress-free in repose, her feet tucked beneath her.

He smiled, then put the coffee cup on the end table. A second later, he picked up the cup, and put a coaster beneath it. There. Peter would be proud.

Then he found an afghan, and draped it over Ellie, tucking the knitted plaid blanket lightly around her frame. He dimmed the lights and left the room, Sabrina still on his hip.

"Looks like you're stuck with me, kid," he said to the baby. She laid her head against his chest again.

Apparently, she didn't mind. And for the first time since Dalton had found the kid in his living room, he didn't mind so much, either.

CHAPTER NINE

ELLIE scrambled to a sitting position, in a panic. The baby. Where was the baby?

For that matter, where was she?

Then the room began to come into focus, the pieces assembling themselves in her mind. The leather sofa. Mahogany table. Stone fireplace. She was in Dalton's house. On Dalton's sofa.

Dalton?

Oh God. She hadn't. Ellie racked her brain, then relief hit her. No, she hadn't. Still, where was Sabrina?

Ellie got to her feet, running a hand through her hair, and padded through the darkened downstairs rooms. "Dalton?"

No answer.

"Sabrina?"

No answer on that end, either.

Ellie headed into the kitchen, but that room was as silent and empty as the living room. A single light burned over the sink, but that was it. No one in the dining room or bathroom—not that she'd expected anyone there.

That left upstairs. Ellie hesitated a moment on the bottom step, listening, but she heard nothing. "Dalton?"

She took one step up, another, then a third, calling his name every few steps. Finally, she reached the landing, and the first bedroom on the right. The door was slightly open, but she paused to knock against the door frame. "Dalton?"

She heard him stir, then call her name in a way that seemed so soft, so intimate, it was as if they were married, and she had just come home at the end of a long day. Come home to him. "Ellie."

"I…I, ah, woke up and I was…" She forgot what she wanted to say. Forgot why she was here. Forgot everything except the fact that she was standing outside of Dalton Scott's bedroom, acutely aware he lay a few feet away.

"You were here," he finished for her. She entered the room the rest of the way. He was sitting up in his king-size bed, against stark white sheets and a stack of white pillows. A thick dark comforter lay over the bed, seeming to invite her in. But most of all, there was Dalton, bare-chested, and very, very sexy.

Whoo.

She inhaled, but couldn't seem to let the breath go, nor catch the next one. "How….I mean…why am I still here?"

"You fell asleep on the sofa. I didn't want to disturb you. I'm sorry, I probably should have left you a note." He slid off the bed and stood. Much to Ellie's relief—and a little disappointment—he had on a pair of sweatpants. He crossed the room, his eyes seeming so much larger and darker, more mysterious, in the near dark of the room. "You were like an angel, laying there. It seemed a crime to make you move."

"Where's Sabrina?"

"In the room across the hall. Sleeping in the portable playpen." The darkness draped around them like a blanket, cozy and soft, drawing her closer. Enticing her to enter his bedroom, but she held her ground, even as she wanted to slip into his arms and feel his warm skin against hers.

"How did you get her to sleep?"

He had winnowed the gap between them, and now, Ellie really couldn't breathe. She could barely even think. "She must have been as sleepy as her mother, because she fell asleep on my chest."

"She did?" Surprise raised the notes in Ellie's voice. "And you…well, you let her?"

Dalton might have thought she hadn't noticed, but Ellie had. The way he remained standoffish with Sabrina, how he tried not to hold her too long or too close. How he avoided opportunities to play with her.

He was a competent babysitter, simply not an involved one. She'd chalked it up to inexperience, to him being a guy, to him not knowing Sabrina very well.

But deep down inside, Ellie knew there was something more. Something that circled around to Dalton's problems with writing emotions in his novels. What that was, Ellie didn't know.

Told herself she didn't want to know, because that would entail getting closer to him. Getting to know him, seeing inside his heart.

"The kid's not so bad," Dalton said with a shrug. "She's got a cute little laugh."

Ellie's jaw dropped. "You made her laugh."

"I played a little game of Peek-a-Boo." He shrugged, like it was no big deal, but Ellie knew it was. A very big deal. This meant Dalton had done more than tend to her daughter's basic needs—he'd *interacted* with Sabrina.

"Peek-a-Boo."

He grinned. "Are you going to repeat everything I say tonight?"

"I just can't believe you did that. I mean, all you've done is feed her, and rock her. Lay her down for a nap."

He narrowed the gap even further, one hand sneaking around her waist, pulling her to his hips. She gasped, her hands automatically rising to touch his chest, warm hard planes beneath her palms. Oh how she wanted to kiss that skin and taste every inch of him. In the dark, his touch became ten times more intimate, more…

Like something a husband would do. Ellie's pulse quickened, her heartbeat accelerated, and her brain sputtered.

"What can I say?" Dalton said. "I guess you two are starting to grow on me."

She'd come over here earlier tonight to lay down some ground rules. No more kissing. No more physical interaction. She was supposed to be keeping her distance, because that was the only way she could do this.

And here she was in his arms, her entire body wishing he would kiss her, wishing they were married, and this was their bedroom, and they were done with talking, and they could just head over to that bed, and end this aching, demanding need inside her.

"Sabrina and I…we should go home," Ellie said.

"It's three in the morning," Dalton replied. "Too late to be waking the kid and then trying to get her settled again. Stay the night."

Stay the night, she thought. Oh, how she wanted

to. But where. Here? With him? Did she dare? Did she want to?

"You can sleep in the guest bedroom with Sabrina," he went on, as if reading her mind. "There's an alarm clock on the nightstand. Fresh sheets on the bed."

"Stay here. With you."

His hand came up to cup her jaw, thumb tracing over her bottom lip. Tempting, oh so tempting. She wanted to curve into his body, to forget every intention she'd laid out earlier, as neatly as the freshly ironed linens across the hall. "With me," he whispered, "but not *with me,* as much as I would like that. Because I'm trying really hard—" and with that, he danced a kiss across her lips "—to be a gentleman here, and I'm not often one. Or at least not a very good one."

She rose on her toes and kissed him, her fingers making waves in his hair. He was warm, and tasted of sleepy desire, the kind that she knew she'd find if she rolled over in bed and woke him up, wanting to make love at some odd hour. "What if I don't want you to be a gentleman anymore?"

He groaned, and his grasp on her waist tightened. "Oh, Ellie, don't…because it wouldn't take much for me to forget all the reasons I had for spending the night in my own bed. Alone." He bent down and kissed her again, this time deeper, harder, longer, his tongue tangoing with hers, raising a heat in Ellie's body that refused to be quenched. "I want you, Ellie, believe me. But you deserve so much more than I can give right now."

Then he broke away, and stepped back into the shadows of his room. "Go to bed, Ellie. I'll see you in the morning. Sweet dreams."

Oh, she'd be dreaming, all right. But she doubted any of her dreams would be sweet. Or about anything but what had just happened.

Dalton spent the rest of the night staring at the ceiling, pretending to sleep. Acutely aware of the woman across the hall, and how close he'd come to having her in his bed.

Damn. He'd either made the best decision of his life tonight or the worst one.

Finally, at six, he gave up on sleep and went down the hall to the third bedroom that served as his office. He powered up his computer, worked a little on his book, following his normal morning routine of writing a scene before getting to the carrot of checking his e-mail. He'd learned long ago that the Internet could be a huge time waster, so the best thing to do was to get some work done—and then allow himself the reward of getting to his messages.

"Good morning."

He spun around on his chair, to find a sleep-rumpled and sexy as hell Ellie at his door. "Good morning." He smiled. "Wow."

"What?"

"You're…gorgeous."

"And you are blind. I look awful in the morning."

"If that's awful, then I need to check my dictionary, because I've been using that word the wrong way." Dalton took a moment to process Ellie's presence. He hadn't had a woman wake up in his house in, well…forever. Odd didn't even begin to describe the sensation, but coupled with that was a nice sense of hominess, of completeness.

Alarm bells clanged in his head. Dalton was treading awfully close to a danger zone he'd vowed to steer clear of.

Ellie stepped inside the office. "What are you doing?"

"Working. Or trying to, anyway. More like buying time until I check my e-mail."

She laughed. "I do the same thing. Only with me, it's coffee. I'd stand there and inhale the entire office coffeepot and not get any work done in the morning if I didn't pace myself."

"If you want coffee, there's a pot right over there." He grinned. "I have the same problem. So

I made it easy, and brought the pot to me. No more excuses to hang out in the kitchen and avoid work."

She laughed, and crossed to the carafe, filling a mug for herself. While she did, Dalton turned back to the computer. Right now he was stuck. He'd come to the scene with the female detective, where she was supposed to react to the horrific crime scene. A murdered family, not one she had known, but an event which brought up a painful event from her past. And thus far, this morning's writing had been—

Terrible. About as emotional as a philodendron.

He typed a few words. Hated them. Backspaced them into oblivion. Typed a few more, hated those twice as much, and repeated the delete. His gaze strayed to Ellie.

"Can I pick your brain for a minute?"

She stopped stirring sugar into her coffee, and glanced over at him, her tousled hair seeming to beg a man to run his fingers through the brunette locks. "Sure. What do you need?"

You. Me. Alone for a long weekend.

Dalton cleared his throat. "If you came across two dead bodies in a bedroom, throats slashed, their guts splashed on the walls, and you'd seen this killer's work before, back when you were—"

She paled. "Uh…what are we talking about?"

"Sorry. My book."

"Oh. You had me worried there for a second. It's a little early in the morning for the whole guts splashed on the walls thing."

He chuckled. "Forgot not everyone lives in my world."

She crossed to him, the carafe in her hand, and refilled his coffee mug without him asking. Dalton sat back, amazed at that small gesture—and how nice it made him feel to be taken care of. How he could get used to that. And how he shouldn't even be thinking about such a thing, not with a woman like Ellie.

"Thanks."

"You're welcome." She pulled up the second chair and sat beside him, sipping at her coffee. "So you want to know how I'd react to such a scene?"

He nodded. "My heroine has been through something similar in her past. So this brings up a lot of really painful memories. She sees the same murder, in her mind, when she walks in and sees this dead family."

"Dalton, I don't know if I can help. I mean, what we've been doing up until now has been pretty simple, but I've never seen anything like that and I don't know anything about crime scenes or murders."

He pushed off from the desk and spun toward her. "You don't have to. Think about it in terms of an experience you have had. Like…" He searched for a word, waving his hand vaguely.

"Like losing my husband," she said softly. Pain marched lines across her face, into her eyes.

What was he doing? Why was he opening this door? Just to write a book? He should back away, stop this right now. She mattered more than some stupid book. "Listen, Ellie, forget I said anything. I'll be fine." Dalton turned back to the computer.

She laid a hand on his arm. "No, really, it's okay. I want to help you."

"You don't have to talk about this."

"Yeah, I do." And in her voice, he heard that she did. She drew in a breath, then let it out. "I haven't talked about this to anyone, not really. Everyone around me has said I need to deal with it. So I can move on."

He waited.

"I need to move on. Not just for me, but for Bri. To do that, I have to talk. As much as I'd rather do anything else." Another breath, in, out, then her gaze met his. "I never told you how he died, did I?"

He shook his head.

"Car accident. Not one of those mercifully fast ones, either." Ellie ran a hand through her hair. "He was hit crossing the street. Heading to work." Her voice dropped into a softer range, grief tempering the words. "You just never know when you're going to die. And for Cameron, it was as simple as that. Some moron on a cell phone running a red light."

"I'm so sorry, Ellie." Damn. Should he let her continue? Or cut this conversation off now, before it hurt her anymore?

But she kept going, as if now the water faucet had been turned on, and there would be no shutting it off. "At first, we thought he'd be okay, but it turned out he had all these internal injuries, and a few days later, he was gone. Thank God we had those days, because at least we could talk about us, about Sabrina. We had those conversations, the ones so many people don't get to have." She lifted her gaze to his and he saw the tears welling in her beautiful green eyes, tears he couldn't make go away, not this time. "At least we got to say goodbye."

"Oh, Ellie…" What could he say? What could he do? He reached for her, but she stepped back, as if saying, *don't touch me now, not yet, not until I've said it all.*

"Cameron left me with a mortgage…and nothing else. No life insurance, no plan. It wasn't his fault, I mean, he was young. Who thinks they're going to die at twenty-nine? He kept meaning to get life insurance, to set up a will, but…"

"It's just not something you think about at twenty-nine," Dalton finished.

"Yeah." She paused a long moment, her gaze in some faraway place, and gestured toward his computer. "It wasn't a horrible crime scene like your heroine had, but it was horrible to me. And it hurt." She drew her gaze back to his, the tears spilling onto her lashes now. "It hurt so bad, Dalton. So bad. I never thought I'd move on. Or get out of bed. Or *breathe* again."

A crack ran through his heart, breaking it like thin ice. He stepped forward, not letting her escape this time, and reached out, taking her hands in his. "Ellie, I wish I'd known. I'd have… well, I don't know what I'd have done, but I'd have done something."

"There was nothing anyone could do. It was all on me." She looked down at their clasped hands. "I had to force myself to get out of bed every morning. To put one foot on the floor. To leave the house. And do you know why I did it?"

He shook his head.

"For her," Ellie said, her voice so soft, the words were a breath. "If I didn't have that baby growing in me, that life on the way, I don't know how I would have made it."

He didn't know how she'd done it, either. What a hell of a woman. He admired her a hundred times more now than he ever had before. She'd gone on after an incredible tragedy, a real life heroine, stronger than any of the women he'd created on the pages of his novels. And she was still doing that every day of her life.

"You're stronger than you think, Ellie. You'd have been fine."

A smile worked its way across her face. "Maybe I would have."

He brought her closer to him. "I'm serious, you would have been fine."

She tipped her chin. "All I know is that having Bri saved me. She got me through a really hard time, but…"

"What?"

"Nothing, really. It's just hard to have a loss like that and a lot of changes afterward." Then she glanced at his computer screen. "So you asked me, how I'd react if I saw a death that reminded me of a horrible death I'd gone through before, and I can tell you, at first, I'd be frozen, all over again. I wouldn't act. Not for a little while. I'd be picturing all I'd lost, and be so afraid of losing that again, even if it wasn't the same situation. There's so much at stake when you get close to someone, but so much more when you lose them. Because you can't ever say those words you meant to say. You can't ever give that hug you wanted to give. Those moments are gone. They're gone." The last words added in a whisper that nearly broke Dalton's heart.

Dalton closed his eyes for a brief second. He thought of all the words he'd go back and say, if only he could. All those words he'd kept to himself and missed speaking, because he'd been young and scared. "I know what you mean."

"But then, after that moment of fear passed, I'd have to act. I'd have to be busy, to have something to do, like a bee flitting from one thing to another."

"Why?"

"Because," she said softly, her voice catching before it regained its regular strident tones, "if I didn't keep busy, if I stopped for even a second, I'd break down and cry. And I…" She paused, and in that pause he saw the Ellie he knew, the one who could do it all, who held a wall between herself and him, between herself and a relationship because she had to protect her daughter above everything else. "I couldn't afford that second."

Dalton had the words he wanted. He had the emotion he wanted. And he had the heroine he wanted.

But she was here, in the flesh, and no longer on his page.

Ellie had gone downstairs to make them some toast, leaving Dalton to write, but he found his fingers wouldn't work. He stared at the screen, and thought about what Ellie had said. How much she'd opened her heart to him.

While he'd sat here and kept his own closed. He'd had his opening—he could have told her why he, too, knew all about hugs that could never be given, words that could never be said.

But he'd chosen only to speak that one lame sentence instead.

He had better avoidance tactics than a covert military operation. Which was exactly why he closed his book file and opened his e-mail program instead. So he could avoid some more. Boy, had he perfected that technique.

"Your breakfast, sir," Ellie said, placing a plate with two pieces of toast, topped with hearty slices of cheddar cheese.

After he thanked her, she took a piece off her plate, then turned away, wandering his office, looking at the titles on his shelf. "I only have a few more minutes. Then I have to get Sabrina up and ready for the day. I definitely have to go in to work today. It's our mandatory Thursday morning production meeting, so no playing hooky or calling in sick to help you write." She paused and turned to face him. "Actually, that's what I came over to talk to you about last night. I know you had offered to babysit Sabrina for only a day or two, until I found someone else, but do you mind watching Bri until whenever Mrs. Winterberry gets back? I mean, I know it's a lot to ask, and I wouldn't even be asking it if the babysitter thing hadn't been such a debacle last night, but—"

"I don't mind."

"Really? I thought I'd have to beg you." She smiled. "I can offer you unlimited dinners for the rest of your life."

The words "rest of your life" seemed to bounce off the walls of his room. Images of her sleeping on his couch, waking up in his house, filling his coffee mug, flitted through his mind. He could have that—

If he was that kind of guy.

For the first time in his life, Dalton wondered—could he be that kind of man? Had enough years passed, had he changed enough that maybe…

He shrugged off the thought. It wasn't like he could experiment with Ellie, and say, "Hey, let's give this a whirl. I'm not so sure I'm cut out for this kind of life, but let's try." What if he wasn't ready? What if he was terrible at commitment?

What if he let her down as badly as he had Julia?

Better to stay uninvolved and let Ellie find someone else, even if the thought of Ellie in another man's arms made Dalton want to crush a car in half. "You can still make the dinners," Dalton said. "I won't turn them down. Bologna wears on you after a while."

"Deal." She smiled, and it seemed like Dalton's entire world righted itself.

Oh, he was in trouble. He kept wrapping himself tighter around this woman, a woman who deserved everything—and he had nothing to give.

A ping sounded, announcing new e-mails. Like being saved by the bell, Dalton took the opportunity to return to his desk. He scrolled through the few dozen messages, until he got to the one he'd been both dreading and expecting. Reuben's. Dalton clicked on the message, and it sprang open, displaying only six words.

THIS IS BRILLIANT! GIVE ME MORE!

Dalton jumped out of his chair, as excited as he'd felt the day he'd gotten the call from his agent, telling him he'd sold his first book. "Yes!"

"What? What happened?" Ellie asked.

He spun toward her, and grabbed her by the waist, hauling Ellie to him. "He loved it. My editor *loved* the new pages. You know, the ones I fixed after we worked on them? I sent them over to him yesterday."

"He did? Oh, Dalton, that's wonderful!"

"And I have you to thank. If it wasn't for you, Ellie, I wouldn't have been able to turn those pages from bad to…'brilliant,' as Reuben called them."

"Well, I'm sure—"

"No, you were the key, Ellie. *You.*" Then he

became acutely aware of her body against his, of the feel of her in his arms. Of how sharing his joy had become something much more.

Something much sweeter. Something he should be avoiding, something he'd vowed to avoid during those sleepless hours last night, but knew he couldn't stay away from her any more than he could avoid eating or drinking or breathing. Time slowed, the world closing in to just the two of them.

"Thank you," Dalton said, his voice low and gruff, his mouth drifting closer to hers with each syllable.

"You're…welcome."

Her eyes were deep, dark pools that drew him in, held him tight. Called to him in a way nothing else ever had. "You know, I don't know if words are enough." He leaned down, and stopped resisting the urges pounding in his brain—and kissed her.

She responded in an instant, curving tighter against him. Her arms went around his back, as if trying to narrow a non-existent gap. Her breasts arched against his chest, and the flame that had been a backyard firepit became an all-out inferno.

Dalton tangled his hands in Ellie's hair, lifting the dark brown tresses with his fingers, letting them slip through his fingers, a silky mahogany waterfall. Then his palms drifted against her cheeks, the warm, soft skin that he had thought of, fantasized about, a thousand times since their last kiss. She'd become nearly the only thing he thought about. Wanted. Needed. Even if he knew he was all wrong for her.

She was soft against him, a perfect fit for every part of him that had been lacking, filling in those dark recesses, those empty holes. The months, the years he'd spent in relationships that had gone nowhere, thinking he could live with this pit in his gut, never needing to fill it—

He'd been wrong.

His hands drifted down, sliding over her curves, along the soft fabric of her sweater, and the silky edges of her skirt. She let out a soft moan, and pressed even tighter to him, their kiss deepening, tongues exploring, tasting, teasing.

Her kiss deepened, the hunger erupting in Ellie, one echoed by his body, multiplied by every taste of her lips, every caress of her skin. He cupped her jaw, and enjoyed every ounce of kissing Ellie Miller.

Thoroughly.

When Dalton finally drew back, leaving one last lingering kiss along Ellie's lips, he knew one thing for sure.

Saying goodbye to Ellie at the end of all this, and going back to being just neighbors who waved to each other across the expanse of fresh-cut grass on Saturday mornings or said hello over their mailboxes on Tuesday afternoons was going to be a hell of a lot harder than he'd ever thought.

"Well, if that's how you thank me for helping you with a few chapters, I can't imagine what would happen if I helped with a whole book." She smiled.

He chuckled, then took a few steps back, giving both of them some distance. "Actually, I was wondering…"

Ellie had crossed to his bookcase, as if the idea of distance appealed to her, too. "Wondering what?"

"What would you think about making this temporary arrangement a little more permanent?"

A look of panic filled her face. It took Dalton a second to realize why, then he replayed his words in his head. "Oh, no, I meant permanent in the way of you working for me. Your help was invaluable. I don't know if I can finish the revisions without your help. So I'd like to offer you a job."

"A job? Doing what?"

"Exactly what you did the other day, and this morning. You help me write the emotional scenes, then you read them over, tell me where I've gone wrong, and give me pointers on how to strengthen my female characters."

She was shaking her head before he even finished the sentence. "I can't quit my job. I need to pay my bills—"

"I don't know if I can pay you exactly what you

make now, but considering you won't be commuting or needing so much childcare, it should work out to about the same."

"I need my health insurance—"

"I'll put you on my plan. Believe it or not, but back when my career was doing well, I made a lot of money, and I was smart enough to put it aside. I can afford this, Ellie."

"We've only worked together once. You have no idea if this would last." She broke away from him, pacing his office, as nervous as a tiger in a cage. "I can't just up and quit my job over that."

"What's the worst that could happen?"

"What's the worst? I could throw my entire life into turmoil for something that doesn't work out. You don't get it, Dalton. I'm a single mother." Ellie stopped pacing and patted her chest. "I don't make decisions anymore on a whim."

He moved to the bookcase, leaning an elbow on the shelf, and waiting until her gaze met his. "But you used to, didn't you?"

"A million years ago, sure. Who doesn't?"

"True."

Hadn't he? Made stupid decisions on the spur of the moment?

And hadn't some of those decisions led to monumental regrets?

Regrets that still weighed on him every night

when he was alone and thought about other paths his life could have taken. Regrets that told him he should have made better choices. Been a better man when he was younger.

"I understand your fears. But I need you, Ellie. I've tried everything short of starting sacrifices in my backyard to get my writing back on track, and here you come along, read some pages, say a few words, and wham—it's like I've found the magic cure."

She shook her head. "I can't take those kinds of changes, I just can't."

"Even if it means you could be with Sabrina every day. Working at home? Instead of leaving her here like you have to today?" He closed the space between them, peering into her eyes, trying to see past the wall she had up, a passel of bricks filled with fears and doubts, and cemented together by a thick independent streak. "With writing, you can make a difference, touch a reader's life."

"How?"

"The words you put on the page, the issues you choose to tackle. That kidnapping book, it generated so much reader mail, I almost couldn't answer it all." He saw Ellie consider his words, and knew she was thinking back over what they had worked on so far, thinking about the characters they had created together, and picturing the way the book might touch a reader. "Most of all, if you worked with me, you'd be here, with Sabrina. Isn't this exactly what you've always wanted to be doing, spending every day with her?"

He saw her sharp inhale of breath and knew he'd offered up the trump card she couldn't resist. She glanced past him, at the second bedroom across the hall, where her daughter lay sleeping, and in her eyes, he saw her torn between the life she had and the life she could have—

If only she'd take a chance on Dalton.

A bet even Dalton Scott wasn't so sure he'd make.

Ellie had just been handed everything she'd ever wanted on a silver platter.

The problem?

It came attached to Dalton Scott, a man who turned her world upside down and inside out every time she came within ten feet of him.

Oh, she could handle working at home, she could handle a change in jobs, she was sure. And he was right, she could definitely see where writing books could hold the kind of touch-the-world work she'd wanted back in college, unlike her current job. But a change from the busy TV station with lots of people to the quiet house with the loner, hermit-like writer—

That was a whole other kind of change.

Not to mention every time she got near Dalton, she didn't think about jobs or earning a living or paying bills, she thought about kissing him. Not exactly a good way to keep that mortgage payment in the bank or food in the refrigerator.

For the first time in weeks, she was grateful for the mandatory Thursday production meeting in Lincoln's office, one no one was allowed to miss, not unless "they were dead or in the process of a dismemberment"—Lincoln's words. The time at the office gave Ellie a good excuse to leave Dalton's house for a couple of hours, along with avoiding an answer to Dalton's job offer. Sabrina had stayed behind with Dalton, who had assured Ellie he'd be just fine getting the baby to play and go down for her morning nap.

"There you are," Connie said when Ellie got off the elevator. "The invisible woman."

"Sorry. At least I made it in time for the Thursday production meeting."

"Oh, I forgot to call you!" Connie said. "Lincoln canceled it." She leaned in, an inquisitive look on her face. "What have you been saying to the man lately? He's been…decisive. That is so not him."

Ellie laughed. "I got tired of going to meetings every five minutes, and when I wasn't at Lincoln's beck and call, I told him to make decisions on his own."

Connie raised a hand in a high-five gesture. "Good for you. It's about time somebody made him grow up."

Ellie laughed and slapped Connie's palm. "Just doing my job, and apparently pulling off a minor miracle in the process."

"Well, good thing you did. You're invaluable around here, El. I don't know what we'd do without you."

"I've been hearing that from all sides today."

Connie took a seat on the edge of her desk and gave Ellie a knowing smile. "From the look on your face, I'd say the other person telling you that is an M-A-N."

Ellie felt her face heat. Geez. What was she, in sixth grade again? "He's a guy, but he's just my neighbor."

"Just a neighbor, huh?" Connie grinned. She reached behind her head and readjusted her red curls into the jaw clip holding her hairdo up. "Is he cute?"

"I suppose. He's tall. Dark-haired. Blue eyes." Ellie shrugged. "If you go for that kind of thing."

"*Hello,* if you have a pulse, you do. And how do you know Mr. Wonderful?"

"He's babysitting Sabrina while Mrs. Winterberry is taking care of her sister. He makes Bri laugh. And he likes picnics. We went on one the other day, just the three of us." She tried to bite back the smile working its way to her lips, but it came all the same. "He's a writer."

"He's sexy *and* he loves babies? Marry him now, Ellie, before the rest of the female population of Boston grabs him. And if he has a brother, hand him over, because I could sure use a good man, or even a half-decent one."

She was not going to discuss dating Dalton Scott and definitely not going to discuss marrying Dalton Scott. Ellie pulled her planner out of her bag and started flipping through the pages. "Tomorrow morning we shoot our first segment for next week's show. Are we all set for the guest? Did you confirm his appearance?"

"Checked and double-checked. I ordered in the soda he likes to drink, and we'll have those bagels he requested here a half hour before he arrives."

"Good. I'll zip down to the studio and go over the lighting and camera angles with the director. And make sure the set is ready, too."

Connie laid a hand on Ellie's arm. "It'll all go fine, just like last week's show. You can relax, you know."

"I'm sure it will. It's my job to worry."

"I know, but…" Connie worried her bottom lip. "What?"

"Never mind." Connie waved her off. "I'm not even going to ask the question."

"Connie, you've known me the entire two and

a half years I've worked here. You can ask me anything."

Connie let out a long breath, then gave Ellie's hand a squeeze. "You look so stressed every time you come in here. I know you're juggling a lot, and Lord knows I wouldn't trade lives with you for all the corn in Indiana, but I guess what I'm wondering is…are you having fun? I mean, any job is worth it if you're having fun."

"Fun?" Ellie let out a little laugh. She closed her planner, already worn so much the binding was threatening to break, and the year was only halfway over. "What's that?"

"Exactly, El. I think you stopped having fun about two promotions ago. And I'm not saying this to talk you out of working here, but I'd hate to see your whole life become about earning a paycheck. When I saw you talking about your neighbor and that picnic, I saw *fun* on your face, and I haven't seen that in ages. I kind of got jealous."

"Oh, Connie, it was just a picnic, it didn't mean anything."

"No, I mean, I realized I hate working here. It's like being a lobster in a boiling pot and every time you try to escape, Lincoln slams the lid on again." Connie smacked the desk to emphasize the point. "You made up my mind. I'm getting out the clas-sifieds at lunch time." She leaned forward. "Do you know what my degree is in? Art. I'm happy painting, not fetching coffee for Lincoln and sitting through another one of his tirades."

"Good for you," Ellie said. "Hey, if any city is great for finding a job in art, Boston has to be it."

Connie nodded, resolve cementing joy on her face. "That takes care of me. Now, what's your excuse for being here so long?"

Ellie shrugged, realizing she had indeed been at the television station for much too long, working for a boss who was demanding and stubborn. A boss she didn't even really like. "I came over here when Cameron did and stayed after he died… because it was easier than facing one more major change. And I kept thinking, eventually I'd find my niche, and I'd find a way to create those stories I'd always dreamed of making."

"Instead, you're catering to soccer players with egos bigger than the Prudential building. And staying here instead of dealing with…well, everything."

Ellie laughed so hard, her stomach hurt. "Yeah, and I'm not any happier doing it than you are. Maybe you should pick up two copies of the paper at lunch."

Connie grinned. "You got it, Ellie. You got it."

CHAPTER TEN

JULIA'S voice hadn't changed a bit in twelve years. When she said hello, Dalton swore he could still hear the sounds of that summer, feel the heat of the sun on the back of his neck, hear the surf pounding against Nantasket Beach, and most of all, feel the weight of his mistakes on his shoulders.

"Julia, it's Dalton."

Silence for what seemed like ten years, but was probably only ten seconds. Still, every one of those seconds passed in agony. The moments hissed by on the phone line. "It's been a long time, Dalton. What do you want?"

He let out a breath. "To say I'm sorry."

If she was surprised, she didn't show it in her voice. Then again, what did he expect? For his apology to be welcomed with open arms, a gushing thank you? For some big Hollywood moment?

Maybe he had. The writer in him had imagined something different. Imagined a moment of quiet reconciliation. Maybe so he wouldn't have to face the uncomfortableness that was coming.

"A lot of years have passed," she said.

"I know. I…well…" He let out another breath. If this was a blank page, perhaps it would be easier to find the right words. Then again, maybe not. "I should have called a long time ago, Julia."

She didn't say anything. That, Dalton decided, was worse.

"And most of all, I should have been there for you more after…after all was said and done."

"You just left." There were no more accusations in her voice, but maybe with time, those had ebbed. On her side perhaps they had. For Dalton, plenty of self-accusations still echoed in his mind.

"When I came home from the hospital," Julia went on, "you were gone, off to college, off on your own life."

"I know." He had left town. Left everything. Thinking that was the easiest way out. But had it been? Had leaving done him any good in the end? It certainly hadn't been the right thing by Julia, not by a long shot. He knew that now, but at the time, when he'd been young and immature—

Well, it had been the young and immature choice.

"I was really mad, Dalton, for a long time, because I felt like you escaped." Years of questions raised the notes in her voice, brought the doubts and accusations swimming back to the surface. "And here I was stuck in that town, dealing with all the stares and the whispers. I didn't have a college acceptance waiting for me afterward like you did. I had a job in a small town New Hampshire deli, where everyone knew what happened to me."

How could he have done that to her? If Dalton could turn back the clock, or travel back in time and speak to the Dalton he'd been then, he would. He'd tell that young man to get a grip, to face reality and to stand up to what had happened, rather than turn tail and run out of town. Because Julia had needed him, and that should have super- seded any fears.

Instead, he'd been a teenage coward, taking the easy way out, leaving town simply because he could while his girlfriend had had to clean up the mess they both had made. Shame and regret warred in his chest, and he wished he was standing before Julia, to offer his apology in person, instead of sitting in his living room hundreds of miles away. "I'm sorry, Julia. I was running away, I guess. I should have stayed. Waited a semester to leave."

"It's all right. It's in the past," she said, her words offering a salve for old wounds. "I understand now. I guess I would have done the same, if I could have."

How ironic, Dalton thought, that he had called to apologize, to close the gap between them, and Julia was the one who was giving him comfort. When really, he owed her so much more than he could even begin to repay. He ran a hand through his hair and tried again, searching for the words—impossible words, really—that would tell her how incredibly sorry he was. How he'd go back and do it all again, if only he could. "I'm sorry, Julia, so very sorry. I should have called you more, been there, come home. *Something*. I was young and stupid, and there just isn't a playbook for what to do when this kind of thing happens before graduation. But most of all, I was really scared," he added, admitting the feeling that had ridden the highest through those years, the one that had driven the wedge between the two of them. "Really scared."

"Me, too." Her voice was lost and small, as if she was eighteen again, and both of them were staring at that pink stick, horror running between them like a river. Their lives had flashed before them—futures shattered, paths suddenly detoured.

Then he finally voiced the words that had waited a dozen years, the ones he kept to himself, because speaking them aloud brought up all the pain of their decision, and brought to life the very thing he thought he could forget.

And couldn't. Not for one second. "Do you ever think about him?"

"Every day, Dalton," she said softly, and her voice broke like glass hitting a wall. "Every single day."

Dalton slumped into a chair. "Me, too."

A long pause. In the background, he could hear the sounds of children playing. Julia's children? He liked to think so. Liked to think that she'd had other children with her new husband, that she had found the peace that had so eluded Dalton.

"Do you think he's happy?" Julia asked.

That was the question that had plagued Dalton most. Kept him up nights for years. Filled him with regret after regret. The one question he couldn't answer. Had they made the right choice? Was their son happy? Healthy? And most of all, better off adopted out to strangers than he would have been with his own parents?

Had he spent the past twelve years laughing and smiling, raised by people who loved him as much as Ellie loved Sabrina? Covered with kisses and hugs, tucked in snugly at night, with the feeling that his world was safe?

"I'm sure he is," Dalton said to Julia, because he knew that was what she needed to hear. And what he told himself every day of his life.

Because it was the only way he could live with

the decision they'd made at seventeen to let someone else raise their child.

Ellie finished out her day, and even though she had given the classifieds a look-over when Connie brought them out at lunch, she hadn't found anything that interested her. There had been pages and pages of jobs that fit her experience and her background.

But only one job offer that gave her everything she wanted.

Along with a few strings she didn't.

She sat at her desk, answering a few more e-mails before she shut down her computer. When she was done, she picked up the picture of Sabrina. "Oh, baby," Ellie said to the photo. "What's the best decision for both of us?"

The weight of making the right choice hung heavy on Ellie's shoulders. Emotionally, she had no doubt that being with her baby day in and day out would be the best option. But financially...

Would it be wise to give up a steady paycheck for one found working for a solo writer? A man who could just as easily decide tomorrow that he wrote just fine on his own, and he didn't need her anymore?

Or was she simply finding reasons not to grab this opportunity?

An hour later, she had finished the daily battle with Boston's stop-and-go traffic, and reached her street. And there, standing in the driveway, was the answer to her dilemma.

Mrs. Winterberry.

Viola Winterberry had seen a lot of stubborn and stupid people in her seventy years on earth, but her two neighbors on Larch Street took the cake. She held Sabrina—Viola could swear the sun rose and set in that baby's face—and stood between Dalton Scott and Ellie Miller, wondering whether these two adults would ever grow up.

"I am taking this little one home with me," Viola announced. She put up a hand before the two so-called grown-ups could interrupt. "The two of you could probably use some alone time, and I know I have missed this baby to bits since I've been gone. And considering I'm going to be going back to my sister's in a couple of days, I want to spend every second I can with my grandneighbor."

That was the word she'd given to her relationship with little Sabrina, a phrase she'd coined to explain how much she loved this little piece of heaven, and how much she looked at her as a member of her own family. Viola's own daughter lived clear across the country in California, which kept her grandbaby too far away for Viola's liking.

So she poured all her excess spoiling into Ellie and Sabrina.

"Mrs. Winterberry, you don't need to do that," Ellie said. "I'm sure you're tired from your trip. Sabrina just woke up from a nap, and she'll be a handful."

"A handful of lovin', is what I say." Viola smiled. "Now let me enjoy my grandneighbor for a couple of hours, and you two go out. Get gussied up. Have a dinner in a real restaurant, not the kind you drive through. When was the last time you did that, Ellie?"

Dalton looked over at Ellie and gave her a grin. "Yeah, when was the last time you did that?"

A flustered flush filled Ellie's face, which suited Viola's purposes just fine. These two might end up growing a brain cell after all. "I don't need—"

"You do," Viola insisted. "Now go put on your nicest dress. In fact—" she ran a discerning glance over his attire "—I think he needs to do the same."

"Why, Mrs. Winterberry, are you saying my T-shirt and jeans aren't good enough to take Miss Ellie out?" He gave her a grin.

"I wouldn't let you take my garbage out in those jeans, Mr. Scott. Now, go make yourself presentable. Ellie deserves to have a gentleman escort her on a date, not some man who looks like a heathen on a motorcycle."

"Date?" Ellie said. "Mrs. Winterberry—"

"I do believe it's time for Sabrina's dinner," Viola said, sliding Sabrina's diaper bag off Dalton's shoulder and onto her own. "Have a nice evening, everyone. And don't worry about coming back too early. I want to stay up and watch the ten o'clock movie." She sent them a knowing smile, then turned toward her own house, marching off before either of them could voice any more objections.

Sometimes, Viola decided as she headed inside, noting Ellie and Dalton still standing on the sidewalk, dumbfounded at how they'd been out-flanked by a woman nearly two and a half times their age, an old dog could teach those young pups a few tricks.

CHAPTER ELEVEN

ELLIE had expected Dalton to do the bare minimum—whatever it took to make Mrs. Winterberry happy, and get her off their backs about going out on a "date." A quick meal at a local diner, or maybe a couple steaks at the road-house around the corner.

Then she saw the limo.

And Dalton in a navy suit, waiting outside the long, silver luxury automobile.

She headed down her stairs, one at a time, her jaw dropping more with each step. "What the…? What are you doing, Dalton?"

A grin curved across his face. "Just following Mrs. Winterberry's instructions."

"I don't remember her saying anything about a limo."

He took a step forward. "She did say something about romancing you."

Ellie reached the bottom step. "No, I don't think she did."

Dalton put out his hand, waiting until Ellie had placed her palm in his. "No? Well, it was inferred."

"I hardly think—"

He pressed a finger to her lips, cutting off her sentence. "I definitely think you are long overdue for a little romancing, Ellie Miller."

Her pulse quickened. She tried to swallow, to breathe, but couldn't. A tremor of anticipation pooled in her veins. Long overdue for romance? Well, that might be, but oh, the trouble a little romance would evoke. She definitely wasn't doing a very good job sticking to her new ground rules. Not at all. So far, she'd violated nearly every single one.

She followed him down and into the limousine, where she was immediately cocooned in a plush leather interior. Chilled champagne waited by their seats, alongside a slim vase holding a single pink rose. Ellie turned to Dalton, awestruck. "You…you thought of everything."

"Just because I can't *write* a romantic scene doesn't mean I can't dream one up." He handed her a champagne flute, as the car started to move. "To an unforgettable night," he said, clinking his glass with hers.

"It already has been." Ellie took a sip, the

sweet golden liquid slipping down her throat with ease.

Dalton leaned forward. His blue gaze locked on hers, holding her as tight as a spider with a web. Then he leaned forward, ever so slowly, and took the champagne from her. He put the glass in the holder, never breaking eye contact, the hold mesmerizing, more intoxicating than the alcohol. "You look amazing, Ellie. The skirt you wore earlier today was beautiful, but this dress—"

"Thank you."

"—is even more incredible, stunning, gorgeous, astounding—"

She laughed. "I get the point. You don't need to drag out your thesaurus."

He cupped her jaw, fingers dancing along the edge of her hairline. "Oh, but I do. Because I don't think even you're aware of how utterly beautiful you really are, Ellie Miller. In jeans, in a skirt. When you're sitting on a park bench, looking up at the sun, or just waking up at my house."

"Is this all part of the plot to romance me?"

He shook his head, slow, his gaze still tight on hers. "It's not a plot, a book, or any kind of fiction at all. It's simply what you deserve. A wonderful night out." Dalton took her hand, the gesture so sweet, so gentlemanly, that it caught Ellie off guard.

They sat together in the back of the limo,

chatting about nothing really, just silly things like the weather and the neighborhood. To Ellie, the small talk was a nice reprieve from the worries about bills and work and the baby. Too soon, the limo slowed to a stop. The bright awning of The Merlot Garden hung in front of them, announcing the entrance to a small Italian restaurant known for its world class wine list and exquisite attention to detail. "I've always wanted to go here."

"A friend of mine owns this place. It's wonderful." Still holding her hand—a wonderful experience in and of itself, and something she hadn't expected—Dalton led her inside the cozy restaurant.

"Dalton! Come in, come in!" A large man in a black suit with a bright pink tie strode forward the instant they entered Merlot Garden. He grabbed Dalton in a quick hug, then released him, affection clear between the two men. "And who is this beautiful lady?"

"This is Ellie Miller. Ellie, this is Jordan Valkerie, the owner. We met in college. He was a miracle worker with a hot plate and a microwave."

"A contraband microwave, I might add," Jordan said with a hearty laugh. "But we won't tell the dean that."

"There was a lot we didn't tell the dean," Dalton added.

The two men chuckled some more, trading war

stories about college, including Ellie in a round of raucous tales about late-night parties, wild pranks, and class cutting, as they walked toward a booth at the back. "Here you are. Enjoy your meal." Jordan waved them in, then disappeared into the kitchen.

Velvet curtains swathed either side of the booth, providing a quiet, private little nook. Soft instrumental music played over the sound system, and a fat vanilla colored candle provided muted lighting. The setting couldn't have been more romantic if it had been a movie.

A waitress came by and took their drink orders, leaving behind a basket of fragrant, hot focaccia bread and olive oil for dipping. "This place is wonderful," Ellie said. She sat back against the seat, soaking up the atmosphere, enjoying simply being out in public, in a real restaurant rather than a kitchen with a jar of baby food in one hand. "Have you come here a lot?"

"Do you mean, have I brought a lot of dates here?"

"I didn't ask…"

"I have been here a lot, but only to let Jordan feed me. But I've never taken a woman here on a date." He gave her a grin. "I couldn't romance you by repeating a scene I'd already written, now could I?"

"No." Once again, a thrill ran through Ellie. But it was quickly chased by questions.

Why was Dalton doing all this? He'd already made it abundantly clear that he wasn't interested in a permanent settling down kind of life. He wasn't the kind of man who wanted to be a husband, a father. And really, she wasn't going to waste her time dating men who had no future in Sabrina's life. Nor was she sure she was ready for more. For a future with another man.

Dalton knew that. Which brought her right back to the same question. Why would he go to all this work tonight, if he had no intentions beyond this evening? In every kiss, she read more than just a night, and yet...

His words said something else altogether.

"Your bottle of Chardonnay," the waitress said, presenting their wine, and two glasses. She poured the golden liquid, then waited for Dalton to taste and murmur acceptance, before leaving again.

"The lobster ravioli here is amazing," Dalton said. "And so is the portobello mushroom lasagna."

Ellie folded her hands over her menu. "Dalton, why are you doing this?"

"I thought you might want a recommendation or two, since I've been here before. But if you want, I can call Jordan over. He's tasted everything."

"No, I meant, why are you working so hard to get me to fall in love with you, if you have no intentions of loving me back?"

The words hung between them as heavy as cannonballs. Dalton placed his menu on the table and slid it to the side. "I'm not trying to do that, Ellie."

"Then what is all this—" she waved at the wine, the candle, the velvet curtains "—about?"

"A nice night out. A nice dinner."

She had to stop fooling herself, stop getting wrapped up in all these fancy details, and be real about what this was tonight. "A pity date for the single mom."

"No, of course not."

She leaned forward. "Come on, Dalton, don't patronize me. I get it, okay? You don't have to sit here and pretend to be all into me, and into this night. We both know how it's going to end."

"Ellie…"

"You're going to go back to your life alone. And I'm going to go back to mine." Ellie drew in a breath, and pushed the words past her throat. Past the limo, the roses and the champagne. "I can't afford to fall for you, Dalton. I can't do that to my daughter or to myself because I know how it feels to lose someone. So don't waste this—" once again, she waved at the table and the romantic fixings "—on me, when you could use it on a woman who doesn't come with so many strings." She grabbed her purse and stood, her heart breaking as she did. "Thank you, though."

"Why are you thanking me?"

"Because for a minute there, you made me remember what it was like to be a woman again. And made me realize there's hope for me to have a life down the road. Life with a man who wants what I want." Her gaze met his, and all those kisses, all those times he'd taken her hand, all those smiles, sank to the bottom of her stomach. "I wished that had been you and I'm sorry that it wasn't. Good night, Dalton. Best of luck with your book."

Then she turned and left, before she could change her mind. And make a mistake she'd regret for not just tonight.

But years to come.

After Ellie paid the taxi driver, she rang Mrs. Winterberry's doorbell, and steeled herself for the lecture that was sure to come. True to form, Mrs. Winterberry gave Ellie a frown when she opened the door. Sabrina lay on the floor in Mrs. Winterberry's living room, wagging a rattle back and forth. "Where's Dalton? Why are you back so soon?"

"I missed Sabrina," Ellie said as she entered the house and dropped onto the floor beside her daughter. Bri looked up at her mother and smiled, dropping the rattle and reaching instead for Ellie's finger, holding tight, as if she didn't want to let her mother leave again. "Isn't that reason enough to come home early?"

"Not when you're supposed to be out enjoying yourself. And especially not when you left here in a limousine and returned in a taxi."

Ellie cursed the large picture window at the front of Mrs. Winterberry's house, and the older woman's tendency to watch the comings and goings of everyone in the neighborhood. "I appreciate you offering to watch Sabrina tonight, Mrs. Winterberry, but Dalton and I…we're not really dating material."

Mrs. Winterberry placed a glass of lemonade on the coffee table near Ellie, then sat across from her in one of the ornate brocade armchairs. "And why exactly is that?"

Ellie sighed. "It's complicated. Suffice to say, we want two different things."

"Or maybe you just think you do."

"We've talked about it. He doesn't want to get married or have kids. He's very definite about that."

Mrs. Winterberry waved a hand. "Men. They never know what they want. You need to *tell* him what he wants."

Ellie chuckled. "I get the feeling Dalton is not the kind of man you can *tell* anything to."

The older woman considered those words for a moment, while she sipped some lemonade. "Perhaps. But still, I think he'll come around."

Sabrina began to blow bubbles and kick, then make herself laugh by her antics. Ellie chuckled, and brushed a kiss over her baby's forehead. "I don't have time for that. Sabrina's my sole agenda."

Mrs. Winterberry placed her glass on the endtable and leaned forward, her face somber. "You make a child your whole world, Ellie, and then one day, you wake up, and the child's grown up and your world is empty."

Ellie glanced at Sabrina, at eight months old, still so needy and demanding. "I'm a long way from that, Mrs. Winterberry."

"Those years go faster than you think, my dear."

The doorbell rang. Mrs. Winterberry rose, a smile racing across her face. "My, my, I wonder who that is." She crossed to the door and opened it, then turned to Ellie. "Look who's come to visit, Ellie. It's Dalton. Looking for *you*."

How convenient. Mrs. Winterberry probably sent Dalton a telepathic message to come right over. Ellie wouldn't put it past her—her neighbor seemed intent on making sure everyone on the block had a happy ending. Ellie gathered Sabrina's diaper bag, slung it on her shoulder, then picked up the baby and got to her feet. "I'm going to take her home now," she said, ignoring Dalton's arrival. "Thank you for watching Sabrina, Mrs. Winterberry. It was nice to get out for a little while."

"Anytime, dear."

"Ellie, I want to talk to you," Dalton said.

"I'm going *home*," she stressed, then brushed past him, heading out the door and down the porch steps. On her shoulder, Sabrina strained, trying to reach for Dalton.

Ellie ignored it all, and just kept going, cutting across the street, digging her house keys out of the front pocket of the diaper bag as she walked. Night had begun to fall, bathing the street in a deep purple glow. Parents were calling their kids to come in, couples were sitting on their front porches, enjoying one last cup of coffee and conversation, while others took the dog on an evening stroll around the block.

"You're just going to walk away?" Dalton said, keeping up with her.

"I already said everything I had to say back in the restaurant."

"Yeah, you did," Dalton said. "Then you left before I got a chance to respond."

"You've made your feelings clear, Dalton. I'm not going to waste my time, or yours." On her hip, Sabrina was bouncing up and down, trying to reach for Dalton. He wasn't helping the matter by wiggling a finger at her. Ellie inserted her key into the lock, opened her door, and entered her small Cape-style house, hoping that would be the hint Dalton needed to leave.

But instead he followed her.

Fine. If he insisted on coming with her, then he'd have to be part of the evening routine. She dropped the diaper bag by the door, then headed for the changing table. Let him see what it was like to be part of life with baby—after all the playtime was over. That would drive Dalton back home.

After all, anytime he had to get too close to Bri, she noticed that was when Dalton made the most of inserting personal space—i.e., he got the heck out of there with some excuse or another.

"Are you going to talk to me?"

"Nope. I'm going to give my daughter a bath and get her ready for bed, then do the same for me."

Instead of going anywhere, he shrugged. "Fine. Then I'll help."

"Suit yourself. But you'll probably end up with a wet suit, and drool on your shoulder."

"I have other suits. And I know a good dry-cleaner."

They weren't talking about baby baths. Or bedtimes. Or anything of the sort. And both of them knew it. They were still carrying on the conversation from the restaurant. Ellie was telling him in no uncertain terms *this is my life, like it or not,* and Dalton was playing the game that he wanted to be a part of it.

Well, Ellie wasn't buying a word of it.

"Don't say I didn't warn you." She slipped off her sweater, then brought Sabrina over to the small changing table in the corner. There, she stripped the baby down to her diaper—something that absolutely delighted Bri, who laughed and bounced—then walked into the kitchen. Unlike Dalton's house, Ellie's was tiny, with all five rooms running right on top of each other.

A few minutes later, she had one side of the kitchen sink filled with warm water, and a naked Sabrina sitting in the silver basin, splashing happily while Ellie wiped her with a soap-soaked washcloth. Dalton took a few steps back. "You weren't kidding about the wet part."

Ellie laughed. "She loves her baths."

"I can see that." But still, Dalton stayed, even moving back within splashing distance. He bent over and picked up a toy Bri had dropped, and handed it to her, giving the plastic elephant a squeeze as he did. The toy's spout released a stream of water, delighting Sabrina, who let out a giggle. She smacked the water, sending a wave over the sink.

And right onto Dalton's shoes.

"I owe you for that, kid," Dalton said, and gave the elephant another squeeze. It sprayed her a second time. "Whoo-hee."

Sabrina laughed, sputtering when some of the

water hit her face, and waited for him to do it again. He obliged her, twice more, even as she laughed and splashed him back.

Ellie watched in amazement. This was so not going according to plan. Dalton was playing with Sabrina? Remaining in the kitchen? Getting wet on purpose?

"Do you want to take over?" Ellie asked.

"Take over?"

"Yeah, with bathing her. I forgot to get a towel and—"

"Oh no, no. You do the bath." He grinned. "Baby rules, remember?"

"Baby rules?"

"You were the one holding her when you put her in the sink."

Ellie laughed. "Not fair."

Dalton took a step closer to Ellie. "I distinctly remember someone else not playing fair a couple days ago. Now I'm soaked," he gestured toward his wet chest, "so I'll go get the towel."

Good. Maybe now that Dalton's clothes were wet, he'd leave and she wouldn't have to tell him all over again why they were wrong for each other. Nor would she have to keep wondering why Dalton could have such a good time playing with Sabrina yet claim he'd make such terrible father material.

"The towels are in the—" Ellie cut off the sentence as she watched Dalton take off his jacket and hang it on a chair. Oh my. He'd looked good in a T-shirt. Incredible bare-chested. And now, in a wet dress shirt, he looked plain sexy.

"Where are the towels?" Dalton asked.

"Uh…" Ellie focused, holding Sabrina with one hand, while the baby continued her two-handed homemade water fountain. "In the closet by my bedroom upstairs. First door on the right."

"I'll be back in a second. Before she soaks you, too."

"Thanks."

Walking through Ellie's house alone gave Dalton an intimate portrait of the woman who had thus far only been inside his house. She had a comfortable house, a very cozy environment. If she lived with him, he realized, this was what his house would look like. Instead of all the hulking male furniture in leather and dark woods, he'd see more of these light tones, soft fabrics and pastel walls.

At the top of the stairs, he reached for the knob to the linen closet, then pivoted, peeking into Ellie's bedroom. He knew he should stay out of the room, and stay in the hall, but before he could turn back to the closet, he found himself stepping into the bedroom, picturing her in the space.

Big fluffy yellow gingham pillows. A white comforter thick enough to swallow a man. And a bed that looked as inviting as a deep, dark lake at the end of a very hot day.

That was Ellie Miller's bedroom. The space, decorated with white maple furniture and a single puffy armchair, surrounded Dalton with a sense of comfort he hadn't found in years, if ever. He had the sudden urge to do one of two things—

Turn around and flee.

And turn around, bring Ellie upstairs and lay her in that bed, and never ever leave this room again.

"Dalton?" she called from downstairs. "Do you have that towel yet?"

"Coming right down." He spun on his heel, leaving the gingham behind. But wishing, in an odd way that he didn't have to.

Ellie had done this on purpose, Dalton decided.

She'd left him to zipper the kid into this sleeper pajama thing, which was pretty much akin to trying to wrestle a snake into a bag. Supposedly, Ellie had had a pressing load of laundry to start, and she'd asked Dalton to do the jammie thing. He'd thought that would be easier than laundry.

Yeah. Not.

It took a good five minutes before he had the squirming baby inside the fuzzy pink pajamas, and the top flap snapped in place. Then he picked Sabrina up, and put her on the blanket Ellie had spread out on the floor. "You could have warned me," he said when Ellie returned.

"Warned you what?"

"That this pajama thing wasn't easy. At all." He sat back on the floor and looked at Ellie, who had plopped a basket of laundry beside her chair. "And that you were going to run out on me tonight."

Silence fell across the room. She ignored him, and instead picked up a towel and folded it. On the floor, the baby kicked her feet up and down.

"Are you done avoiding me, so that we can finally talk about this?"

"I don't see why," Ellie said. "Like I said before, you want something different from what I want. What's the point in taking this any further, Dalton? I'm not going to waste my time falling for a man who only wants me for one thing." Her clear green eyes met his. The fire that had ignited between them on that first day sparked in her gaze. "We can't keep playing this game."

"No, we can't." Although he wanted to keep kissing her, didn't want to stop seeing her, where else was this going to go? It wasn't fair to Ellie, or to Sabrina. But Dalton didn't want to be fair. He wanted it all, damn it. To hell with the consequences.

The baby started her word-song again,

working her way through all her sounds, while she kicked her feet and swung her fists. "Ba-ba-ba. Mu-mu-mumma."

The soft smile stole across Ellie's face again, the one that hit Dalton in the gut every single time. Ellie put down the towel and knelt by her baby. "Say *Mom*ma, Bri. Say *Mom*ma."

Sabrina kicked and squealed. "Momma, momma, momma."

Ellie beamed and looked up at Dalton, the joy on her face wide and explosive. "She said it. *She said it.*" Ellie picked up the baby and held her to her chest, burying her face in Sabrina's, nuzzling the baby's neck. "Oh, good girl, Sabrina, good girl."

Dalton tried to work a smile to his face, to share in Ellie's joy, but something leaden had fallen to his gut. It had been a wonderful moment, an amazing moment.

A *family* moment.

And Dalton had never felt more outside the family than he did right then. And never wanted more to be a part of it. As weird as that was.

This was what Ellie was talking about. This was why she had walked away in the restaurant. Because he only wanted to be involved with her for the sugar on top, and not to be involved with the web of this—

The family. The Momma moments.

He thought of his own son, living with someone else, strangers somewhere in another part of the country, no longer a baby, of course. Dalton had missed the Momma day. Missed the first steps. The first teeth. Missed all of that. By choice.

Had he made the right decision?

He watched Ellie's face now, saw her heart soar as Sabrina repeated the word again, and felt his own chest crack.

Sabrina squirmed around in Ellie's arms. She bounced up and down, using Ellie's arms for leverage, and looked at Dalton. "Da-da-da."

Ellie looked at Dalton.

Dalton stared at Ellie.

"Did she just say what I thought she said?" Ellie asked.

"Nah," Dalton said. "I don't think so."

Sabrina bounced some more. Waved a fist around. "Da-da-da."

Dalton's heart wedged in his throat. He'd definitely heard that this time.

Sabrina had looked right at him and called him Dada. Maybe she didn't mean it, maybe she didn't understand it, but there it was. The one word he'd never heard from his own child, had come from Ellie's baby.

Dada.

For a second, he forgot that he didn't want this.

Forgot that he had vowed to stay away, to keep himself above all these connections. The word echoed in his head, in Sabrina's soft little sing-song. Joy broke inside his chest, a flock of birds taking flight. Dalton wanted to capture this moment, to hold it tight and never let it go.

Dada.

A smile worked its way to Dalton's face and he stared at Sabrina, dumbfounded and utterly captivated by a pair of big blue eyes, two rosy cheeks and one word.

Dada.

"I guess she sees you as…" Ellie paused. "Her father. I mean, you've been around her more than any other man has and well, she just kind of naturally thought…"

"Yeah." Dalton cleared his throat. "Yeah, I guess she does."

But he wasn't Sabrina's father, was he? He could get as caught up in this moment as he wanted, but when it came down to the cold, hard facts, Dalton wasn't Sabrina's father and he shouldn't be playing a game he couldn't finish. Dalton got to his feet, backing up and putting distance between himself and the whole scene. "I better leave."

Ellie rose, too, Sabrina still balanced on her hip. "What are you so afraid of?"

"I'm not afraid of anything."

She narrowed the gap between them, her gaze meeting his, sparking with a challenge, refusing to let him escape this time. "Ever since I met you, Dalton, all you've wanted to do is put distance between me and my daughter. It's like you're terrified of getting close to the baby. Not to mention me. You'll kiss me. You'll flirt with me, but you won't have a relationship with me or with Bri. Why?"

"I'm just not good with kids."

"I don't believe you. I've seen you with Bri. You're awesome with her. And I saw your face just now. You…well, you love her. But you won't get close." She sighed and put the baby back on the floor, handing Sabrina her pacifier and a toy, then went to Dalton. She laid a hand on his arm, her touch soft, concerned. There. "What happened to you, Dalton, to make you this way? Because I know something did. I see it in your writing. It's as if you're leaving something out. Like there's a wall up, a line you won't cross. Why? What's made you so afraid of getting close to people, not just in real life, but on paper, too?"

He turned away, crossing to the window, looking out over the street where he'd lived for several years, among dozens of families. In a huge house that could have held the very thing that he'd always wanted, and never dared to have for himself. Why choose this neighborhood above all others? Was he just torturing himself? "Not all my books were like that. My first one had no walls. No boundaries. I poured everything into it. Hell, I poured my *soul* onto the page."

She waited, quiet and patient. Behind them, the baby suckled the pacifier and began to nod off.

"I had all these pent-up emotions sitting there, waiting, I guess. They'd had nowhere to go for years, and when I sat down to write my first book, it all poured out on the page. It was almost…cathartic. Almost." He shook his head at the irony, then went on. "That was the book that launched my career, that hit the *Times* list, and made me 'Dalton Scott.'" He used little air quotes. "But for all that book did, it hurt like hell to write it, and I vowed I'd never ever write another one like that again."

"Why?"

He spun back around, and in his eyes, she saw the pain that Dalton had held back all this time, as if a veil had finally dropped. "Because every word was like ripping off an arm. Because that one might have looked like a thriller on the surface, to my editor and my readers, but underneath it all, it was my story."

She thought a second back to the pages she had skimmed on his shelves. "That's the book about the father whose baby gets kidnapped. He basically turns up heaven and earth to find him."

Dalton closed his eyes and nodded. "For me, that book was really about—" he let out a long breath "—my own son."

The words hit her like a freight train, and took a long second for Ellie to process. "You're… you're a father?"

"My son—" and saying those words a second time seemed to release something in Dalton, cut a weight on a fishing line that had held him down for so long "—is twelve now."

"Oh, Dalton… Where is he?"

"I wish I knew." His gaze went back to the window. Could his boy be one of the dozens sleeping in the houses peppered among the neighborhood? Or did he live in Seattle? Denver? New York? Every day Dalton wondered what he looked like, whether he liked baseball or football, if he had siblings or a dog, silly questions, and serious ones.

Most of all, Dalton just wondered…

Was he happy? Was he with people who loved him?

But he had never voiced those thoughts, thinking it would hurt too much. Dalton had thought sealing off this part of his heart would make it easier, but if anything, he wondered if maybe it had made it harder. Had he done himself a disservice all this time?

Had he been wrong?

"His mother and I gave him up for adoption after he was born," Dalton said. "It seemed like the only decision we could make. We were seventeen, still in high school when she got pregnant, and…I don't know, scared as hell."

"Oh, Dalton." Ellie went to him then, both arms wrapping around his chest, holding him tight. Understanding. Caring.

But he couldn't accept the embrace, not yet. Not until he'd said it all. Told her everything. "I shouldn't have done it," he said. "I should have tried. I should have—"

"You were young, Dalton. You didn't have a choice."

"There's always a choice, Ellie."

She reached up and cupped his face. "You're right, there is, but that doesn't mean it's always the *right* choice. Look at me, I'm an adult single mom with a college degree raising my baby, and I'm still struggling. What kind of home would you have been able to provide as a teenager?"

"I loved him, though." Dalton's voice broke, shivered on the last syllables. "Maybe it would have been enough."

"You loved him enough to make the right decision," she said softly. "A chance at the best possible life, one with two parents, who would love him and be there for him."

He shook his head, the questions that had plagued the last dozen years still raising their ugly heads, still knocking on Dalton's heart. "I worry about him every day. Wonder where he is. If he's happy. If he—" The sentence sliced in half.

"If he thinks about you."

The lump in Dalton's throat was too thick for him to speak. He nodded instead.

"Of course he does." Ellie's touch echoed gentle words. "You should sign up for that adoption registry. So that when he's old enough, and he wants to find you, he can. And you can answer all his questions, and maybe he can answer all yours."

"Do you think…" Dalton shook his head and cut himself off, his gaze going to Sabrina, only now he couldn't see the baby anymore because his vision had blurred, because so much had happened in the last few minutes, too much for his heart to process, and the swirl of emotions nearly overwhelmed him now. "Do you think he'll ever forgive me?"

"I think it has to start with you forgiving yourself." She pressed a hand to his cheek. "A child is a gift of love, Dalton, and you made the most incredible gift of all to one lucky couple. Stop beating yourself up."

There, Dalton knew, lay the problem. Forgiving himself had always been the biggest roadblock.

He may be able to say all the right words. Write them on the page, but telling them to himself—

That was where he got stuck.

"I tell myself that, but there are still a hundred questions in my mind, Ellie. A hundred more regrets." He turned back to her, his voice hoarse. "And until I answer those, I don't know how I can be any kind of man for you or—" his gaze went to Sabrina again and now, his voice did crack "—father for her. I'm sorry."

CHAPTER TWELVE

WHAT Dalton had told her explained everything. His distance with Sabrina, his unwillingness to get close. Ellie watched him cross the street, a solitary, hunched figure in the amber light of the streetlamp.

Dalton Scott was a man with a shattered heart. A man who couldn't forgive himself for a decision he'd made as a teenager, a decision anyone could understand and support.

Ellie had never met a man she admired more. He had made an incredibly difficult choice, one she wasn't so sure she could have made, not now that she had had her own child, and known the joys of holding her baby.

A little while later, Ellie had Sabrina fed and tucked in bed. If Ellie had any sense at all, she'd be doing the same. But instead, she paced the house, puzzling over the day. Over Dalton Scott.

And over the reasons why she hadn't gone after

him when she'd had a chance. Because for all her understanding of what he'd said and why he'd acted the way he had, she was still standing in her own house. Alone.

A little after ten, her doorbell rang. Ellie expected to find Dalton on her doorstep, but found instead—

Mrs. Winterberry.

"Turn your TV to Channel Three, please," the older woman said, as she entered the house, her bag of knitting over one arm, and her house slippers in the other hand. She paused by the door long enough to take off her shoes and exchange them for the slippers.

What on earth? "Channel Three?"

"The commercial's about to end, and I'd hate to miss any of my movie." Mrs. Winterberry crossed to the sofa, sat down and plopped the knitting bag down beside her.

"Isn't your television working?"

"Of course it is. But I can't very well watch my grandneighbor from my house, not if she's already asleep in her crib."

"You don't need to watch her, Mrs. Winterberry. Not tonight."

"I do if you're going to go across the street and settle things once and for all with our handsome neighbor." Mrs. Winterberry shook her head while she tugged out her knitting needles and a half-finished red and white sweater. "Honestly. The two of you are so stubborn."

"We're just…"

"Stubborn." Mrs. Winterberry propped a fist on her hip. "My dear, when you get to my age, you'll learn that life is too short to sit around waiting for a man to come back across the street and decide he can't live without you. You want him, you go get him. And stop being so afraid of changing your life."

Clearly, Mrs. Winterberry wasn't going to go anywhere, not until Ellie did first. She handed her neighbor the remote, and flicked on the television. Channel Three popped into view, with an advertisement for carpet cleaning playing on the screen. "For your information, I'm not afraid."

Mrs. Winterberry arched a brow.

Was she? Ellie thought for a second. Had she been as at fault in all of this as Dalton? Had she been holding back, holding her heart secure, using the excuse of "complications," because she was terrified of being left alone all over again? All this time, she hadn't dealt with losing Cameron, because she'd been afraid it would hurt too much. Then little by little, being around Dalton had forced her to do so. And it hadn't hurt nearly as much as she'd thought.

So what was she afraid of now? A little change?

"Go," Mrs. Winterberry said, giving Ellie a little wave, using the needles to emphasize the point. "And don't worry about hurrying back. I have a whole lot of knitting to get caught up on, and tonight's movie is a double feature." She grinned, and Ellie could swear she saw a gleam in Mrs. Winterberry's light blue eyes.

Dalton sat in his office and realized he was an idiot.

Of course, he'd probably been an idiot the entire week. It had just taken the last few minutes for the truth to come out. As it did in most things with a writer, the truth had bled through his fingers and onto the page.

He watched her walk away, and felt something tear in his chest. She disappeared into the rain, swallowed up by a powerful storm. But it wasn't the storm that took Ellie away, it was his own fears. His own silence.

He hadn't said what he needed to say when he'd had the chance, and now he hadn't just lost the woman. He'd lost the family he'd sought for years. All these years, he'd thought he'd been looking for his child, seeking his face in that boy on the bike, or that child in the mall. But really, all he'd wanted was the dream of a family he'd had to let go because he'd been too young to handle the mistake he'd made at seventeen.

And now, the words lodged in his throat, too late.
I want you. I need you.
I love you.

He popped out of his chair, and backed up.

He loved her?

He thought of the last few days. Of the picnics. The smiles, the toast, and of all things, the coffee.

And Dalton had almost thrown it all away.

But how could he make this work, how could he be the kind of man she wanted, needed?

He glanced out his window, at the little Cape across the street, that housed two women he loved, and thought—

How could he not?

Ellie didn't even make it halfway across the street.

"What are you doing here?"

"Looking for you," Dalton said. A smile curved across his face, and Ellie's heart turned over. "What are you doing?"

She smiled back. "Looking for *you*. Mrs. Winterberry is watching Sabrina."

"So that means we're alone?"

Streetlights and porch lights, along with the occasional smattering of landscape lights, punctuated the dark night. A burst of laughter came from a nearby house, announcing the presence of neighbors. A sprinkler system sent its staccato rhythm of water spraying across a lawn two houses down. "As alone as you can get in the middle of the street."

He chuckled. "True." He put out his hand, and hauled her to him. "As much as I love your kid, I'd really rather not have an infant audience, or any audience, right now."

Surprise rocketed through Ellie. Had she heard him right? "You…you love my kid?"

"Sabrina has…grown on me. She's also puked and peed on me, but she kind of made up for it with the whole da-da thing."

It took a half a second, but then the word processed in Ellie's brain. She stared at Dalton, reading his ocean-blue gaze, unable to believe what she'd heard. "You…you just called her Sabrina. Instead of kid."

He grinned. "I did, didn't I?"

She nodded, dumbfounded.

Dalton gave Ellie's hand a tug, and turned toward his house. "Come on inside, Ellie. Let's not have this discussion in front of the entire neighborhood."

As soon as the door shut behind them, Dalton gathered Ellie into his arms. He cupped her jaw, his fingers catching a few loose tendrils of her hair. "I've been an idiot."

A smile curved across her face. "Now there's a first line I've never heard."

He laughed, then sobered, his gaze holding her captive. "I almost let you go because I thought that would be the best thing for both of us. I didn't want to hurt you, didn't want to let you down."

"Oh, Dalton, you couldn't—"

He put a finger on her lips. "Let me say this." He drew in a breath, as if searching for the right words. "Ever since Julia and I decided to put our son up for adoption, I've felt like a failure, like I let him down. And that made me feel like I could never be a good father to another child. Or a good husband. But after tonight, after you and I talked, I went home and I did what I do best to work through my problems. I wrote."

"You wrote?"

"Yeah, and this time, it was good stuff. I'll probably never use it in a book, because this wasn't fiction, but I did let all that internal angst out on the page." He held her face gently and searched her eyes. "My son went to a loving family, I'm sure of that. The agency we placed him with was a really good agency. You were right. Julia and I never would have done right by him, not at seventeen. But now, I'm nearly thirty. I can do a much better job."

She nodded. "You can, Dalton. I've seen you."

His gaze sought hers. "If it's not too late."

She shook her head, a smile breaking across her

face. Her heart soared so high, hitting the clouds, she thought it might never come back to earth. "No, it's not. At all."

"Wonderful." He leaned in, and brushed a kiss across her lips. "Because I don't just love Sabrina. I love you."

Now her heart broke through the clouds, and the smile on her face seemed to become endless. "You love me? But we hardly know each other."

"It was the toast. And the coffee. And the way you smiled. And definitely the chili."

She laughed. "The chili? And coffee?"

He kissed her again, this time longer and sweeter. "In fact, Ellie, I don't want to spend another moment without you or Sabrina in my life. I don't even want you to walk back across that street." He paused, his gaze searching hers, then holding hers. "Will you marry me?"

Marry him? Had he just *proposed?*

Suddenly, fear gripped her. This was moving so fast, maybe too fast. All the what-ifs slammed into Ellie, and she broke out of Dalton's arms and stepped back. "We should take this slower, Dalton. Maybe take a breath."

"You're scared."

"Of course I'm scared. In the course of a few days you've asked me to quit my job, told me you loved me, and now asked me to marry you. You've turned my life upside-down between Monday and Thursday. This is insane, Dalton. It doesn't happen this way."

"You don't have to quit your job. Work part-time. Work half-time. Work eighth-time, I don't care. Just be with me. I just don't want to wait. We're not kids, Ellie. And I've been a fool, putting my own life on hold for all these years, because I thought it was the right thing to do." He took her hands in his. "You've put yours on hold long enough, too. It's time you had the dream you've always wanted. For you and Sabrina."

A tear fell down her cheek. But this time, she wasn't crying from frustration or stress, like when she'd first met Dalton. It was a tear of hope. She could have what she'd always wanted. What she had dreamed of for her daughter. Dalton had showed her that this week.

If only she was brave enough to reach out and take what he was offering, brave enough to open her heart again. Brave enough to welcome the feelings that had been knocking at her heart for days. Ellie lifted her gaze and looked into Dalton's deep blue eyes. "I love you, too," she said softly. "And I can't imagine going back across the street without you either." She took in a deep breath, then let it out. "Yes. I'll marry you."

He grinned, then swept her into his arms and

kissed her, thoroughly and deeply. This time, they walked on the clouds together. "Then let's go home," he said, "and get our daughter. It's time we made a family. Together."

EPILOGUE

VIOLA sat in the church wearing her best hat and a new dress, holding Sabrina, who also had on a new white dress trimmed with a pink ruffle that Viola had insisted on sewing herself. Outside, fall leaves fell from the trees, as if God had decided he'd create his own orange and yellow confetti for the celebration.

"I'm so glad you were there for me," Penelope said, grasping her sister's hand. "Whatever would I do without you?"

"Oh, you'd get along. You have Lenora, you know." Their youngest sister lived in Arizona, but was closest to Penelope, who had always doted on the baby in the family.

Penelope waved in dismissal. "Lenora is a pain in the butt. She talks too much."

Viola chuckled. "Now, shush, Penelope. The wedding is about to start."

"You really should stop interfering in people's

lives," Penelope said, adjusting her wide-brimmed yellow hat. "Although you did bring me my Harold—the cutest doctor on the third floor, and right at retirement age, which was mighty handy for me. Now you need to find someone for yourself."

"Pish-posh. I'm fine. I have my daughter, my granddaughter, and my grandneighbor." She brought Sabrina to her chest and placed a kiss on the eleven-month-old's forehead. "That's enough for me."

Penelope just hmmed.

At the head of the church, Dalton stood at the altar, handsome in a black tux, looking ready as any man to get married, not a trace of nerves on his face. On one side, stood his eight sisters and two of Ellie's friends. On the other, Dalton's brothers, and the husbands of Ellie's friends. The wedding party alone took up a good portion of the guest list.

The wedding march began. Viola rose, pivoting toward the back of the church. Ellie, resplendent in a simple white gown with a scoop neck, started her walk down the aisle, on the arm of her proud father. She joined Dalton at the altar, and twenty minutes later, they were married and sharing their first kiss as husband and wife.

"You have a father now," Viola whispered to Sabrina.

"Dada," Sabrina said.

"Yes," Viola said. "A momma and a dada. Those are all the words you need to know, little girl. Now your world is complete." She pressed a kiss against Sabrina's forehead, then handed her off to the happy couple when they paused by her pew, creating the perfect ending.

The very one that Viola had imagined when she'd first left Sabrina at Dalton's house. That day, she could have, of course, chosen any of a number of the stay-at-home mothers who lived on Larch Street, but she'd never tell Ellie or Dalton that.

"Thank you, Mrs. Winterberry," Ellie said, her smile warm. Dalton reflected the same smile.

"You're welcome," Mrs. Winterberry replied, then wished them well as they left.

Ellie and Dalton headed up the aisle of the church, their daughter between them. Dalton leaned over and brushed a kiss against his wife's forehead. "She thinks we don't know."

"Should we ever tell her?"

"Nah. My mother wants to meet her," Dalton said. "I've still got all those single sisters, remember? If Mrs. Winterberry can work her magic with them, Sabrina will have some cousins in no time."

Ellie danced her fingers up Dalton's neck. "I was hoping to work on a little brother first."

He wrapped an arm around her waist and swooped her gently against him. "That, Mrs. Scott, is a story we'll start writing right away." Dalton gave Ellie a short but sweet kiss, just a preview of what was to come that night, before releasing her again. She laughed, her eyes dancing with desire and happiness.

And with that, they walked out of the church and into the first chapter of their new life, one that both of them were sure would be a bestseller.

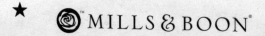

His passions were as tempestuous as his temper...

Even though Kate Whittman was young and inexperienced, she wanted moody Texas rancher Jason Donovan more than anything. But he offered her only brotherly protection.

So Kate pursued another fantasy – becoming a successful New York fashion designer. But just when it seemed that her fairy tale was coming true, fate brought her back to Texas. And to Jason.

Available 1st May 2009

www.millsandboon.co.uk

THREE POWERFUL SEXY MEN WHO CAN'T BE TAMED...

THE HIGH-SOCIETY WIFE
by Helen Bianchin

THE BILLIONAIRE BOSS'S FORBIDDEN MISTRESS
by Miranda Lee

THE SECRET BABY REVENGE
by Emma Darcy

Available 15th May 2009

www.millsandboon.co.uk

FREE

2 BOOKS AND A SURPRISE GIFT!

We would like to take this opportunity to thank you for reading this Mills & Boon® book by offering you the chance to take TWO more specially selected titles from the Romance series absolutely FREE! We're also making this offer to introduce you to the benefits of the Mills & Boon® Book Club™—

- ★ **FREE home delivery**
- ★ **FREE gifts and competitions**
- ★ **FREE monthly Newsletter**
- ★ **Books available before they're in the shops**
- ★ **Exclusive Mills & Boon Book Club offers**

Accepting these FREE books and gift places you under no obligation to buy; you may cancel at any time, even after receiving your free shipment. Simply complete your details below and return the entire page to the address below. You don't even need a stamp!

YES! Please send me 2 free Romance books and a surprise gift. I understand that unless you hear from me, I will receive 4 superb new titles every month for just £2.99 each, postage and packing free. I am under no obligation to purchase any books and may cancel my subscription at any time. The free books and gift will be mine to keep in any case.

N9ZEE

Ms/Mrs/Miss/Mr...Initials ....
BLOCK CAPITALS PLEASE

Surname ....

Address ....

....

....Postcode ....

Send this whole page to:
The Mills & Boon Book Club, FREEPOST CN81, Croydon, CR9 3WZ